MIDNIGHT METAMORPHOSIS

MIDNIGHT METAMORPHOSIS

Daughter of Prophecy Book 1

by

Deborah E. Kehoe

2018

Published by Evertype, 19A Corso Street, Dundee, DD2 1DR, Scotland. *www.evertype.com.*

This is a work of fiction. All the characters and events portrayed in this book are fictitious, and any resemblance to real people, or events, is purely coincidental.

A catalogue record for this book is available from the British Library.

ISBN-10 1-78201-214-1
ISBN-13 978-1-78201-214-6

Typeset in Sabon and Blue Island by Michael Everson.

Cover design by Michael Everson. Photograph "Face from sky" by Branislav Ostojić, Belgrade | *dreamstime.com/vukvuk_info*.

Printed and bound by LightningSource.

Contents

MIDNIGHT METAMORPHOSIS

Chapter 1

Avery

As I stepped into the hallway, I looked down at the piece of paper in my hand and promptly ran right into someone. I reached out to grab her as she flew backward, her books tumbling to the ground. The hand holding my class schedule was caught in a soft grip.

"I'm so sorry!" I said, my face flushing in embarrassment. The girl I ran into was small, shorter than my 5′5″ by a couple of inches. She was rather pretty, with soft brown hair and bangs cut straight over her brown eyes. She had a light dusting of freckles all over her face and arms. When I looked closer at the arm I had hold of, I thought I noticed an interesting pattern to the freckles. There were four or five spots grouped together, creating a larger freckle. It was kind of odd, but not ugly.

"That's okay," she said, picking up her books. "It was my fault, I wasn't looking where I was going." Her voice was so quiet that I had to lean forward slightly to hear her.

"Well, neither was I," I said, laughing slightly as I handed her another book. I glanced down at the paper I still held in my hand. First period English, room 106. "I don't suppose you know where room 106 is?" I asked her. "Today is my first day at Dover. They gave me a map, but

I think I'm already late for class." Nothing like walking in late when you were the new girl. A feeling I knew only too well.

"That's actually my home room, too! My name's Ana, what's yours?"

"Avery." I held out my hand and when she looked at me, put it down quickly and reached out to pull at my sleeve. I offered a shy smile. "Do you mind if I follow you to class?"

"Sure," she answered. "It's right down the hall this way." She turned to the right and started forward. Now that I knew where I was going I took the chance to look around.

The school was pretty new, or at least well kept. The hallway was painted a regular beige, but had a broad black stripe running down the center of the wall, horizontal to the walkway. I felt like it was a large arrow leading me to my class. As we walked, Ana and I exchanged the basic where are you from, what year are you, and ended with comparing our class schedules. We realized that they were almost exactly alike, with the exception of my fifth period being gym and hers was Algebra.

We arrived at class. As we walked in the door, all the students were standing around and talking loudly to each other. I noticed a blonde girl all the way across the room seemed to be holding court to a handful of boys and girls. She stopped talking as I walked to the front of the room and everyone else grew quiet as well. Ana, took a step away from me and walked directly to an open seat in the middle of the class. I had to do the new girl thing and hand my schedule to the teacher at the front of the class.

The English Lit teacher, Mr. Newsome, was a large man, and by large I'm talking tall, not round. He was probably

6′4″ with a lot of white hair that grew over his ears, curling every which way. I didn't think he was as old as the white hair made him out to be. His face was unlined, except for wrinkles around his eyes, which I hoped meant he smiled a lot.

"Class, it looks like we have a new student," he said. In the hushed room, his voice sounded too loud. "Avery, why don't you introduce yourself to the class," and he gestured for me to move forward into the room.

Great. I hated these introductions. There must have been thirty students in this classroom. My stomach fluttered as I imagined each individual stare landing on different parts of my body. The girls were all sizing me up, and the boys were probably guessing my breast size. I crossed my arms instinctively across my chest imagining what they were all seeing. I was just an average girl. My hair was a dishwater blonde, with some darker brown lowlights, at fifteen, I had no breasts to speak of, so I'm sure that was some disappointment to the guys in the room. My mom had always said that she developed later, around sixteen. *You could only hope*, I thought as I glanced around. My birthday wasn't too far away, falling on Halloween. Staring at the class I raised an eyebrow and blushed, maybe there would be a miraculous development. My eyes were hazel, turning brown or green, depending upon my mood. They were brown when I was uncertain or nervous, like I was right now.

I looked out the wall of windows on the far side of the room into the quad below. There were picnic benches set up under the trees and I imagined kids hung out in the square during lunch and between classes. A half hour ago when I had gotten to school there were kids sitting at those tables even though the grounds were covered in fog giving the school a gloomy feel. As I stood in front of the class,

I noticed that the fog still hadn't lifted and I shivered. I twisted the gold ring I wore on my right hand thinking back to when my mom had given it to me only a few weeks ago. I looked down at it while I gathered my thoughts. The initials GC glinted on the gold shield and I drew comfort when I remembered my mother telling me that it had belonged to my great-grandmother, whom I had never met. As I twisted it I felt it tingle on my finger, and I don't know if it was my imagination but it felt like it was sending a pulse of energy into my hand. I looked up at when the room lightened as the sun broke through the fog. *That's weird*, I thought, noticing how the sun fell on four people in the room. Myself, Ana, the blonde girl holding court across the room, and a boy sitting in the back of the room, wearing a blue hooded sweatshirt, with a piercing through his right eyebrow. My mouth was probably hanging open as everyone in the class moved in slow motion, except the four of us. I snapped my mouth closed and we all looked at each other, and then looked at the now frozen students around the room. I heard Ana take a deep breath, the blonde girl said, "What the hell?", and I thought, *WTF is more like it!* The cute boy in the back of the room cleared his throat.

I jumped slightly and everyone started moving again. I looked at the boy, and he gave me a slow nod. The teacher gave me an impatient look. *Just get this over with*, I thought to myself. "Okay…" I said my voice quavering, "my name is Avery Anderson. I just moved from Oklahoma yesterday and I'm living with my aunt. She owns Come Sit a Spell on main street?" My voice trailed off and I glanced sideways at the teacher hoping that short synopsis was a good enough introduction. I cleared my throat. "Is anyone sitting in that seat?" I said hoping to stop him from asking questions. I pointed at an empty seat in front of Ana.

The teacher glanced over at Ana, looked puzzled for a moment and glanced at his seating chart. "No, that seat seems to be vacant," he said. "Go ahead." He then glanced at Ana and looked at the chart for her name. "Miss, uh Brookes, may I speak with you a moment?"

In a daze, I looked around at everyone moving at normal speed and sat in the empty seat slowly placing my bag on the ground. I looked around at the other students again, assuring myself things were back to normal and reached for a notebook and pencil out of my bag. I noticed that Ana and the teacher seemed to be having a minor disagreement. I heard Ana say kind of loudly, "I've been here since school started, I can show you my notes!" The teacher looked confused but seemed to take her at her word and she moved back down the aisle and slumped back down in her seat.

"What was that about?" I asked, glancing up at the teacher who was double checking the seating chart again.

"He doesn't remember seeing me here before," she said. I noticed she had a notebook in front of her with English Lit written on the front. She had been in the class before her notebook was full of notes. I shrugged it off as other than annoyed she didn't seem to be really concerned about it.

"Did you notice what happened before?" I asked her trying to keep my voice down while Mr. Newsome was writing something on the board at the front of the class.

"Yeah, that was really weird!" She exclaimed.

"It was!" I said. *I'd sure like to know how and why that had happened*, I thought.

I looked over at the pretty blonde girl a few rows over. I nodded my head towards her and whispered, "What's up with blondie over there?"

"That's Summer. She's pretty cool." *That seemed to be an understatement*, I thought. Girls and guys were trying to get her attention, but she was staring at Ana and me, totally ignoring the kids talking to her. She got up from her desk and moved over to stand by the seat right next to mine. Someone was already sitting in that seat, but she set her bag next to it and looked at the girl with a smile on her face. "Sugar, why don't you move over to my old seat, the light is better by the window and it will really show off that pretty face." She spoke with a slight southern accent, which seemed really out of place in Southern California.

Mr. Newsome faced the class as Summer sat down and stretched her hand out to me, "Avery, I'm Summer, what the hell just happened?" I was about to reply with a "Hell if I know," however, Mr. Newsome started his lecture. The class was reading Shakespeare's Romeo and Juliet. Thankfully, I read that in my Sophomore English class and it wouldn't take much for me to catch up. I grabbed that book out of my bag, looking for the correct page.

Summer whispered, "What period do you have lunch?" I held up three fingers. "Me too," she whispered. "Let's get together." I looked at Ana, "Lunch?" I knew she and I had the same lunch period. I liked her, and since she was also "lit up," I wanted her in on the conversation as well.

"Sure." she whispered. Then she looked to the front of the class and started taking notes.

I smiled, feeling hopeful, maybe this new school won't be so bad if I've already made a couple of friends. Remembering what had just happened, I looked around at everyone. *They seemed normal*, I thought, then tuned back into the lesson. They were studying the fight scene in the first part of the play. Before concentrating on the lecture, I tucked my head down and snuck a glance over my right shoulder through my hair at the boy in the blue hoodie. He was staring straight at me. Normally I'd get flustered and turn around, but our eyes caught and held, mine widening slightly. He was totally cute! He had dark brown hair, almost black, with a cowlick that flipped his hair up on the right side of his forehead. His skin was lightly tanned as if he spent a lot of time outside, and he had dark eyes that looked more purple than blue. He raised a pierced brow at me in question. Embarrassed, I flushed lightly, but I casually tucked my hair behind my ear and looked back towards the front of the class ignoring him, for now.

Chapter 2

Cole

The hood of my sweatshirt was uncomfortably bunched up between the back of the chair and my neck. As I reached back to straighten it out, the door to the classroom opened. A girl walked through who looked slightly familiar. I was puzzling out how I knew her when a slightly taller girl walked through the door after her. The first girl walked to an empty seat and sat down, while the other girl talked to Mr. Newsome at the front of the class. Everyone in the room stopped talking and stared at her, including me. I could feel my heart pulse pick up. *Interesting*, I thought to myself.

I checked her out while she was talking to the teacher, noticing her hair first. It was a cool dark blonde, but with really dark brown streaks running through it. Mr. Newsome cleared his throat, "Class, we have a new student. Avery, why don't you introduce yourself to the class."

Avery. The name gave me a jolt in recognition and I straightened in my seat. As she spoke briefly to the class, the room stilled, and by stilled, I mean everyone started moving in slow motion except myself, Avery, Summer, and that other girl that walked into the class with Avery. In the next instant I was surrounded by a soft glow of light. I could feel its warmth on my body, generating heat, but I didn't feel my temperature rise noticeably. My pulse sped up more as I locked eyes with Avery. She raised her eyebrows looking surprised. I nodded at her and cleared my throat startling her. That seemed to break the moment, because the light diminished, and everyone started to move again as if nothing had happened.

This had to be her, I thought, rubbing my damp hands across my jeans. My mind raced with instructions and possibilities. I watched her as she took her seat and noticed Summer getting up from her assigned seat across the room to switch with another girl. She, Avery, and the other girl spoke softly and nodded at each other.

If this was her, I thought, *how was I going to work my approach?* Avery gave me a quick glance through that cool hair, and our eyes caught again. She held my gaze for a minute then looked back up at the teacher. I reached up to the barbell in my eyebrow and gave it a tug. When my finger hit the barbell, I sent a small jolt of electricity through it, feeling its tingle make the hair on my neck stand up. I stretched out my fingers and popped my knuckles, letting the air roll between my fingers like I was moving a pencil. I shrugged off the current and tilted my head forward to listen to Mr. Newsome's lecture. *I could take some cues from Romeo and Juliet*, I thought. My eyes swept Avery's body, noticing her sweet curves and delicate features. *She is cute*, I thought.

When the bell rang I met up with Ben in the hallway. We bumped fists and walked towards our lockers. He and I had gotten pretty close since I moved here, being on the same soccer team. Ben was an amazing goalie, with an incredible reach.

"Dude, that physical was lame. I got a little closer to Nurse Ratchet than I wanted," he gave a small shiver. He leaned up against the locker next to mine and watched me open the lock. I touched the dial and it started spinning to the right on its own. The wind moved the hair on my head and a piece fell forward. I quickly brushed it back. The lock finished spinning and I opened my locker.

"You passed, though, right?" We had a big game coming up next week and we needed our star goalie.

"Absolutely!" Ben ran a hand through his sun-streaked hair, leaving it sticking straight up. "I wouldn't mess up our chances against Oxnard, don't worry!" He glanced lazily around the hallway. His attention caught by a girl walking down the hall, her hips swaying gently. A tail peeked out from under her jacket and twitched. Looking back at me he asked, "Did Newsome give us a load of homework?" He looked slightly worried.

"Nah, but you did miss the new girl," I said, putting my books in the locker and slamming it shut. Not looking directly at Ben, I put my hands in the pocket of my hoodie and we started moving down the hall.

"Cool! Is she hot?" Ben looked around like he was trying to spot her.

"What do you care? You've been hooked on Summer since that party on the beach in August!" I bumped him against the wall with my shoulder, and when he bounced back continued, "She's all right." I said, downplaying her looks. "The interesting thing about her was this thing she did with the room when she entered." I told him about the light spotlighting the four of us and how everyone seemed to be in super-slow motion.

"Dude, that's awesome! Man, I wish I hadn't had to deal with the Nurse." He shuddered again. "You'll have to point her out to me at lunch."

"It shouldn't be too hard, Summer moved her seat close to her, so I wouldn't be surprised if they were buds already." Ben and I approached my next class. "Let's meet up after next period and we'll scope them out."

"Do you think she's like us?" Ben raised his eyebrows and wiggled them slightly.

I shrugged, but I had a feeling she was exactly like us. "I don't think she'd be going to school here, if she wasn't, but I guess we'll find out."

"Cool." With a hop in his step, Ben moved off down the hall towards his class, joining up with some of the other guys from our soccer team as they opened a door down the hallway.

I took my phone out and sent a quick note to my dad before I entered the classroom.

Three Years Ago

Right before my thirteenth birthday, my father came into my room and sat down. I had been doing some homework, but at the serious look on my dad's face, I sat up and put my pencil down, straightening from a slouch.

"Son, I have some things I need to go over with you." My father looked at me with a serious glint in his eyes and I nodded without answering.

My father and I had gone away to the mountains together for some additional element training. My father was an elder on the Elemental Committee. As an elder, he and the committee were responsible for making decisions for all Elemental families in our city. My father was not the head of the committee because he was only able to control two elements, Earth and Air. However, holding two powerful elements is rare, so that has given our family a level of prestige that we wouldn't have otherwise had. We live in a nice house and have a lot of land for training. My father didn't always have time for getaways, so I had been surprised and pleased when he said he wanted to take a weekend trip together. Of course, I couldn't leave my schoolwork behind, so I was trying to catch up on homework before my training this afternoon.

"Son, before your mother died, I made a promise to her." I kept my face relaxed, but inside I jolted from excitement. My father never talked about my mother. She died when I was small, and any reminder of her could set him off on a really bad mood.

"She wanted you to have a normal childhood, for as long as possible. I'm afraid that with your thirteenth birthday next week, that time has come to an end. I need to explain to you the journey that we are about to take. The mission that we have been given." My father frowned and took a step further into the room.

I raised my eyebrows in surprise, my eyes tracking him. Journey? Mission? Since my twelfth birthday, when I inherited my powers, I had been on a strict training schedule. Working daily with my other friends at school, switching instructors when I quickly outgrew their strength. I had thought that I would go on learning those powers and then, like my father, eventually work towards being on the committee.

My father looked out my bedroom window and I followed his gaze, noticing the wind gently moving the leaves in the trees. He shook his head slightly, straightened his shoulders and faced me again. My eye was caught by movement in my peripheral vision. The tree branches started to bend in the wind, which had suddenly increased, showing my father's agitation.

"You know of the prophecy?" I nodded my head. We learned about the prophecy when we were children in school. A female child born of an Elemental and Seer will, on her sixteenth birthday, gain powers so huge tipping the power balance between our kind. Those powers would be so strong that she will be able to send the powerful Daïmon, Avdar, back to his dimension.

At my nod, my father started pacing the room, his shoes making no sound on the thick carpet. He turned, facing me directly. "Mathis and I have been talking about what to do about his daughter Avery. She and her mother have disappeared from Oklahoma City, and he has lost contact with them. He's very worried." My father stopped and ran a hand through his dark hair. "Diana, his wife, was supposed to wait for him to return, but since she's gone, he's not sure if the Daïmonids have caught up with them."

My father and Mathis had been close since childhood. When Mathis first met his wife, Diana, my father told me that it was he that Mathis confided in. Since the separation of the Elemental and Seer kind, it had been against the law to even walk on the same side of the street as a Seer. Mathis, with my father's help, met his wife secretly, eventually falling in love. When they decided to face their parents, intent on telling the truth about their relationship, their parents were horrified. Diana's mother, a great Seer, had a vision many years ago, which foretold of an end to peace between Seers and Elementals. Until that vision, we had lived together in cities, cohabiting and living side by side, friends with each other. Because that vision was so vague, the heads of the two families, Seer and Elemental, made the decision to separate, discouraging their family members to no longer be friendly with each other.

The reaction of their parents was so drastic, that with my father's help, they made plans to run away together, assuming new names. The prophecy that everyone had kept secret, you see, had possibly begun. Diana was pregnant with their child, and in order to keep them safe, they had to run.

At first, Mathis, Diana, and their child were happy, but their life wasn't easy. Mathis, having three elemental powers, had been counted on by his family to raise them out of poverty. Diana had inherited only the ability to tell if someone was telling her the truth, which was a small power in an otherwise strong matriarchal line. Their positions in society had been very different. After Avery was born, they were happy for a time, but Mathis's guilt over not helping his family started to eat away at that happiness. There were also factions within the Elementals that wanted them caught and tried. Wanted their child to be raised in a controlled setting and watched until she turned sixteen. The fact that they couldn't settle anywhere didn't allow them to keep jobs for very long. As soon as they felt hunted, they had to move, and move quickly.

Mathis had secretly kept in touch with my father. He convinced Mathis that if he came back, he could rise up in rank to become very powerful, and in that way, he'd be able to protect Diana and Avery. Maybe someday, he could bring them back home. So, when Avery was six, Mathis and Diana decided that Mathis would return to the Elemental community and work towards that solution so they could all be together again. Unfortunately, when Mathis showed up without his daughter, the Elemental and Seer Committees refused to advance him, even though he was very powerful. He had to work to gain the Committee's trust and respect. Years went by without his family by his side. He was now a powerful Committee member, as was my father, and they were still the best of friends.

My father paced towards me, "We will be moving to Dover, California, where Diana's sister Brenna just moved. If Diana and Avery make contact, the committee has decided that you are to be her Guardian, ensuring that she reaches her sixteenth birthday." My father looked at me nervously, rubbing his hands together. "If she is the girl prophesied, our instructions may change, but right now, we are just going to keep an eye out for her. Are you ready? I can't stress enough the importance of success. This is our family's chance to prove ourselves. Do you understand how important this opportunity is for us?"

"Yes, sir." I nodded my head, my heart filled with pride, thrilled to be a part of such an important mission and prove myself to my father. "Sir, you can count on me."

Chapter 3

Avery

Ana and I exited our second-period Biology classroom talking about the subject of the term papers we were going to have to write. Unlike in English class, Ana showed a real excitement for this subject, talking rapidly waving her hands around in enthusiasm. I rolled my eyes, it was not my favorite subject, but I nodded agreeably when she looked at me for a reaction. Ana looked so pretty and unlike the kind of plain girl I had first met, that I looked more closely and noticed the color in her face. Wait, what? Movement on her arm had me glancing down at it in surprise. I could've sworn that the freckles I had noticed on her this morning were gone and she now had a peach tint to her skin. She was actually quite beautiful. I noticed a guy walking down the hall stare at her, and just about walk into a pole. I nudged Ana and laughed. I thought she'd laugh too, but she looked really uncomfortable and stopped talking about our Biology class. Then I noticed a kind of crazy thing; the freckles that had disappeared came back and seemed to swirl slightly. The peach tone to her skin disappeared and turned a normal beige tone. She was still sweet looking, but not a knockout like she was two minutes ago.

"Ana, what the heck just happened to you? It's like looking at two different people!" I grabbed her arm and turned it over, looking at her normal freckled skin. I realized something strange had just happened, but her skin can't change colors can it?

"Hurry, up, we're going to be late to meet up with Summer." Ana pulled her arm away from me and brushed off my question. She picked up speed leading the way to the cafeteria, following another one of those stripes of black running along the wall of the building. As we got closer to the cafeteria we joined up with another hallway that had a red stripe running along its walls. The black stripe and the red stripe led into a large room that was the cafeteria. The red stripe on the right, the black stripe on the left, until they joined together on the wall facing the door we had entered through in a wave of black and red. Dover High Fighting Lions was scrolled around the wave, with a picture of a snarling Mountain Lion painted in the center.

"Avery, over here!" My attention jerked away from the snarling lion on the wall. I looked around and saw Summer waving to us from the front of the food line. I smiled and waved back looking around. I saw a small table out of the way and Ana and I went over to take our seats. She and I had both brought our lunches and didn't need to stand in line to get hot food. I glanced over at Summer and waved at her to come join us when she was done.

As Summer walked towards us, I noticed that her stride was long and smooth and even though every student she walked past tried to catch her attention, she ignored them all, carrying an overloaded tray and dodging and weaving through people like it was an obstacle course.

"Let's go eat outside," she said, and kept walking past us through the doors, without a hitch in her step. The cafeteria opened directly out onto the center quad. There were tables scattered around, and a few large trees, providing shade to sit in. She headed towards one of the trees on the other side of the quad. As she sat down on the grass, I looked at the tray of food she carried.

"Hungry much?" I joked. Her tray was full of what looked to be every food item served inside. There was a plate of spaghetti and meatballs, a turkey sandwich, some chips, an apple, and a large brownie. This was not a plate of food that you thought you'd see a tall, blonde Amazon girl with the perfect body eat.

"I've got practice later," she said shrugging as she reached for half a sandwich. Ana had told me earlier that Summer was the star forward on the Dover High girls' soccer team. "So, what's your story?" she said to me as she took a bite. I repeated the same two sentences I had told my first period English class. Summer swallowed her bite nodding slowly and look over at Ana. She frowned slightly and asked, "Are you new, too?"

"No." Ana gave a frustrated growl. "Summer, you and I have gone to school together since you moved here a few years ago."

"Really. Well, that's just strange." Summer looked at Ana as if trying to place her then glanced back at me and shrugged. "So, you're living with your aunt, right? Where are your parents?"

As I was about to answer, the cute boy from home room walked up, his hands shoved into the pockets of his blue hoodie his gaze on me. Next to him was another boy I hadn't seen before. He was just a little bit taller than myself, with blonde hair and green eyes. His hair had gel in it creating little spikes around his head. He had a huge grin on his face and I couldn't help but smile back at him.

I looked back over at hoodie boy. “Hey,” he said with a casual nod and I smiled ducking my head to look at my lunchbag.

“Hi.” I said quietly, glancing at Summer to see her reaction.

Summer seemed surprised to see them both standing there, but shrugged, turning to me, “Sugar, these boys are Cole,” she nodded at the boy in the blue sweatshirt, “and Ben.” She smiled up at Ben and patted the ground beside her. Ben sat down and reached over for the other half of her sandwich. “Hey!” She swatted at his hand.

Cole still stood there looking down at me. Summer said, “Well, have a seat! Avery was just about to tell us how she ended up at Dover and why she was living with her aunt.” Cole took his hands out of his pockets and sat down on the ground next to me. Uncomfortable, I noticed he hadn’t brought any food to eat.

I opened up my lunch bag and glanced inside at a wrapped sandwich, some chips and a couple of sugar cookies. I wanted to avoid their eyes while I thought about what to tell them. Talking about my mom’s death was really hard, but I knew people would find out some way or another, so it might as well be from me. “Well, my mom died in a car accident a few days ago.” I choked up as I said the words and Ana reached over and touched my hand. I tried to smile through the knot in my throat.

“I’m so sorry Avery, that’s rough.” She said softly. I glanced down at her hand, which was still lightly touching mine. Her freckles swirled and then disappeared. I noticed her hand was turning a soothing yellow color. She noticed me glance down, and quickly removed her hand from my arm. *There’s definitely something different about this girl*, I thought.

"Thanks," I said, battling the tears forming in my eyes. I didn't want to become emotional so I took my sandwich out of the bag. It was cut in half so I offered the other half to Cole, "It's just turkey and Swiss, but I'm not really hungry if you want half." He smiled slightly and took half of my sandwich. When he looked down at the sandwich to take a bite, I snuck a look at the piercing in his eyebrow. It was a silver bar with some Celtic scrollwork in the shape of a shield. He caught me checking out the piercing and raised his brow at me again.

Embarrassed to be caught staring again, I quickly looked away and thought about the last time I saw my mom.

I walked into the kitchen pulling my sweatshirt down over my head. My mom was at the stove, scrambling a couple of eggs for breakfast. She reached over and laid her hand against my cheek, then reached back to help me pull my hair out from under the neck of my sweatshirt. Smiling, she turned back to the eggs pushing them around in the pan.

"I have to run up to Chandler today to deliver some kits to a store that's going to start selling them." She said, turning to split the eggs between two plates on the counter. She set them on the table and sat down in the seat across from me.

Taking a bite of my eggs, I chewed cautiously, my stomach churning with dread. At least once a week my mom and I had this conversation. "If anything happens to me…" We both started the sentence and trailed off smiling nervously at each other.

"I know you think it's stupid, but I really want you to take this seriously." My mother pointed her finger at me and swallowed her eggs. "Yesterday I heard from someone

I used to know, from before your father left us. He said that they are coming." At those words, my skin prickled.

"Who's coming?" I asked the question, my voice cracking. Why I asked, I don't know, she never gave me a straight answer.

My mother and I exchanged a look until I glanced away scooping up another bite of my eggs. "Okay. They're coming." I repeated, my voice skeptical. My mom had been paranoid about people "coming" for us, for the last few years but no one has come and I'm starting to believe they never will come, but I kept playing along in order to take that nervous look out of her eyes.

My mother nodded in relief. Her eyes relaxed and she pushed a curl of her brownish red hair behind her ear, her mouth tilting up in a half smile.

"This trip to Chandler is going to be my last trip, but those kits should generate some income for a little while." She said.

After a few years of working as a waitress my mom started making survival kits for hikers. A backpack containing bandages, dried food packets, thermos, survival blanket, ponchos, work gloves and anything else you'd need to survive the end of the world. All of her paranoia has started to pay off and some of the local stores have started picking them up to sell. She nodded towards my backpack leaning against the wall by the door.

"My contact said we have a couple of days, and we need this money. But if something happens," My mom stopped talking until I looked up from my plate and looked at her. I tried not to roll my eyes. Here we go with the secret spy stuff. Her "contact" is a mystery to me, but mom brings him up when she's trying to make a point. Before I had decided if I wanted to raise the subject about this contact, she gave me a fierce look and then changed subjects abruptly, looking down at my hands. "Where's your ring?" She asked sharply.

I looked down and cursed inwardly, fumbling in the pocket of my jeans until I pulled it out. I jammed it on my finger, twisting it until I got it over my knuckle. I looked back up at her and winced. My mother isn't very sentimental and I'd been surprised when she had given me this ring a couple of weeks ago. As usual, she hadn't told me too much about it, just that it was my great-grand-mother's and the ring was really important. I twisted it nervously and my mom reached out and grabbed my hand, stopping the movement.

"Don't take it off again," she said, gripping my hand tight enough that the ring cut into my finger.

"Ouch!" I exclaimed, trying to withdraw my hand from hers. "Okay! I won't!" I shook my hand out and my mother relaxed back into her chair. What was that all about? I wondered. *My mom's paranoia seems to have gotten worse*, I thought.

I pushed my chair back from the table and stopped by her side. "Mom, I'm sure everything is going to be fine. Stop worrying so much." I said, trying to reach down to give her a hug, but she shrugged me off. My chest tightened with hurt, but I pushed that aside. My mom wasn't ever going to be the type to hug. I don't know why I even tried. I have a few memories of my mother when my dad was still with us. She smiled a lot and I felt so loved, she held and hugged me a lot back then, but that was a long time ago. I held a breath and let it out slowly trying to ease the tightness in my chest.

I put my plate in the sink and went over to the door to pick up my backpack. Trying to ease her mind, I smiled and unzipped it to show her the extra set of clothes I'd put in it the other day.

"See, I've been listening to you," I said, pulling a t-shirt out. My mom smiled in relief and I felt a warm glow of pleasure at making that smile appear even if just over a t-shirt.

"I'll see you later." I said with a slight wave and walked out the door.

I had been halfway listening to my teacher ramble on about the Louisiana Purchase when the door opened, interrupting his monologue midstream. The principal, Mrs. Kendrick, stood at the door with a cop next to him. I hunched my shoulders in panic when the teacher looked over at me and waved me up to the front of the room.

Chills raced up my arms as I quickly grabbed my bag, my mom's words from that morning entering my head. Had something happened? I could hear all the other kids start whispering as I walked up the aisle to the front, but I only had eyes for the principal, who had a worried look in her eyes.

"Avery Anderson?" When I nodded, Mrs. Kendrick clasped my arm and led me outside the door of the classroom. The cop followed and huddled next to the principal. She had taken off her uniform hat and had it under her arm. She awkwardly reached out and laid a hand on my arm in what was supposed to be a comforting gesture, but I reached for the strap of my backup shrugging off her arm.

"Is it my mom?" I asked quickly, my heart hammering inside my chest. "Did something happen?" Before the cop could respond, Mrs. Kendrick nodded.

"I'm so sorry honey," she said trying to reach out to give me a hug, numbly I allowed it for a minute until she turned to look at the officer and gave him a nod.

"Your mom was in a car accident this morning. I'm so sorry, but she didn't survive." The officer spoke softly and I glanced at the ground, her words repeating in my head.

"Where?" I asked glancing up quickly, the tears in my eyes clouding her features. I flashed back to the conversation with my mother this morning and her statement about someone coming after us. *I should've paid more attention*, I thought as I brushed the tears out of my eyes.

"Avery, your mom was in Chandler at a stoplight that malfunctioned. All of the lights turned green at the same time and multiple people were injured." Through the tears in my eyes, I could see the cop looked confused.

"Did a lot of people get hurt?" I asked with a tremor in my voice.

"Just one other, seriously, a man on the side of the road was hit by flying debris." The officer's voice faded when he saw the question in my eyes.

"There was a wild wind storm that kicked up suddenly. We think that contributed to the malfunction." The officer continued to speak to the principal as she asked a couple more questions. I realized that they had grabbed hold of my arm and were leading me down to the main office. My legs were trembling, and my mind was racing as I tried to grasp what had happened.

My mom had been right? Was there a connection between someone trying to get us and this accident? I focused when I heard my name being repeated a few times and a hand patting my arm.

Mrs. Kendrick had steered me into her office and was asking if there was someone she could call. I remembered my mom's instructions and told her that I could go to a neighbor's apartment. After giving her a phone number, she called and reached Mrs. Gonzalez who was going to come to school and pick me up.

I reached for the tissue she held out to me and wiped my eyes.

When I came back to myself, Summer and Ana's faces were shimmering with tears, and Cole had put his sandwich down in his lap. I cleared my throat feeling a flush rise up my neck. I sniffed and wiped the tears quickly from my cheeks as I tried to casually go on, my voice trembling as I started. "My mom left me a letter saying I had an aunt in Dover, so I hopped on a bus and got into town yesterday. I didn't even know I had an aunt. My mom never talked about her, but she seems pretty cool. She has that shop off Main that sells tea and stuff." I stopped speaking because Summer and Ana both nodded as if they knew her.

"Your aunt is Brenna Cameron?" Summer asked. She looked like she was about to say more but Cole gave Summer a direct look and she said instead, "My mom is a fan of her tea's." She smiled as Ana nodded in agreement. "Anyway, if y'all don't mind, let's talk about what happened this morning in first period." Summer looked at Ben, "did Cole fill you in?"

"I'm sorry I missed it. I was in the Nurse's office this morning. The season starts next week and I needed to pass the physical." He shuddered comically and continued, "So, everyone was in slow motion? How'd you do that?" He looked directly at me while grabbing Summer's apple and taking a bite out of it.

She smacked him in the arm again and said, "Hey, I have practice later!"

"Me? I didn't do anything!" Shocked, I looked around at the group. "I was just standing there and then the room just slowed down. Well, except for the four of us and did you notice we were all lit up like a spotlight was on us, too?" It was weird, I agree, but why would they think I did anything?

I noticed Cole checking out the gold ring on my right hand. "I saw you twisting that ring around your finger when it happened, can I see it?" Nodding, I tried to tug the ring off my finger, but it wouldn't come loose and I gave up tugging on it.

"Sorry, I can't get it off my finger." I told them about my mom giving me the ring a few weeks ago, and when I mentioned that it had been my grandmother's, Cole sat up a bit and reached for my hand. When he touched it, I felt a small shock again and it turned loosely on my finger, and he pulled it off. "Weird," I said, "I haven't been able to get that off since my mother died."

"What does the GC stand for?" he asked. Cole was turning the ring over, looking intently at the engraving.

"I'm not sure, I think it's someone's initials, but she didn't tell me whose." I said and held out my hand for him to drop the ring back into it. "It's nice to have something of my mom's. We didn't have a lot." I could feel myself tense up against the tears that were welling and rushed to put the ring back on my finger. There was a flash of light and small bolts of electricity flew out and zapped the four of them. I jumped in astonishment. What the hell had happened!

Ana gave a small squeak, scooting back on the grass, but Summer moved closer saying, "What the heck?"

Cole shrugged it off, looked at Ben and said, "Cool."

Ben agreed with a nod to Cole saying, "Awesome!"

I didn't know what to say other than a shocked "sorry!" and thankfully the bell rang for fourth period.

Chapter 4

Avery

I stopped at the sidelines and walked over to the water cooler. As I filled my cup, I watched Summer take a pass from one of the other players and run up the sideline. *Wow*, I thought. *She's amazingly fast*. Summer moved the soccer ball from foot to foot, making it seem as if the girl guarding her was standing still. A defender came forward to block. Summer pushed the ball to the right and whirled around her, coming out of the spin behind the defender, receiving her own pass. She touched the ball quickly with her right foot and drilled it into the net with her left. Some girls cheered and a few came forward to slap her on the back acting like her speed was completely normal. I yelled out a cheer and Summer looked at me with a grin.

I was trying out for an open spot on the team. One of the midfielders broke her leg at practice yesterday by stepping in a gopher hole walking to her car after practice. When I told Summer that I used to play soccer, she suggested that I come out to practice and talk to the coach. I wasn't sure if it was a good idea, I mean, I hadn't played in a few years, but the coach ran me through some drills and talked to me about my conditioning. My skills were a little rusty, but Summer told the coach she'd work out with me and help me get back into shape.

Summer ran towards me from the end of the field and I filled a cup with water and handed it to her. "You're really fast!" I said.

"Yeah, speed runs in my family," she said as if that run was totally normal. She drank the water down quickly and pointed to the football field where the boys' soccer team was practicing.

"Check them out," she said. I followed her gaze and noticed Cole setting up for a shot on goal. Ben, the goalie, was hopping from side to side, mouthing off to him. I could just make out his words, "You know you're not going to get one by me, Cole. You might as well quit trying." Cole grinned and flicked his fingers out at him, a dust devil, filled with fresh blades of grass, twisted towards Ben as Cole took the shot, the ball sailed towards the right corner of the goal. Ben, his t-shirt whipping around him and blades of grass slicing towards his face, took a giant leap from the opposite side of the goal. *He shouldn't have been able to save that shot*, I thought, but he swiped a hand out and palmed the ball, scooping it back out towards a player on the other side who dribbled it back into a line of players waiting their turn to shoot. As he turned back towards Cole, I could've sworn I saw his eyelids fold up together over the center of his eyes, but he blinked and it was gone so I thought I must've imagined it. The wind died down, and the grass settled back onto the ground. Of all the strange things about that save, what struck me was that Ben made it while not wearing any gloves. I said as much to Summer, she grinned and said, "That boy has great hands." The way she said it made me wonder if we were still talking about soccer, but the boys' soccer team did finish last year with a 12–0 record, so I let that comment slide, figuring I'd get the full scoop later.

I saw Ben and Cole laughing with each other, and when they high fived I noticed their hands stuck together slightly. Cole said something to Ben as he pulled his hand away, wiped it off on his leg, laughed, and walked back to get in line to take another shot.

As I turned back to Summer, about to comment on how fast the wind had blown up, our coach blew his whistle and we fell in line behind some other girls to run a couple of laps to end practice. *Boy, I need to get in shape quickly*, I thought, breathing heavily.

"Avery, stop by my office tomorrow for your uniform," the coach said. He was marking something off in his notebook. "You're on the team."

"Sugar, I knew you had skills!" Summer nudged my arm as we ran down the track and I smiled at her, but as she passed by me my smile died.

This was the first time I'd felt happy in years and it took losing my mom for me to feel this way. I mean, I know that I can't live in the past, but I feel so guilty! It was nice to just be normal. I sighed and picked up speed to catch back up to Summer, who was, of course, leading the girls around the track.

After school, when I didn't have practice, I started working in my aunt's tea shop. The shop not only sold tea, tea pots, cups, saucers and other tea items, but also had a few little garden tables where you could "Come Sit a Spell" and have hot or cold tea and a snack. The overall feel of the shop was very soothing and feminine, but there were shelves full of books and magazines that customers could borrow, so we had both female and male customers frequently stay in the store for an hour or so. The tea bins were full of Darjeeling, Chamomile, Earl Grey and other familiar brands, but there were also special mixes that

Brenna created out of different plants, herbs or flowers from her garden. We had regular customers who came in weekly for Brenna's special mix of Sleepytime or T-Eaze. The purpose of the first was obvious from the name, and the second was to help soothe muscle pain or arthritis. Brenna promised that she would teach me about herbs and their natural properties for healing when I showed interest in her special brews.

It was a Thursday afternoon in mid-October when I opened the door of the shop and entered, the smell of black tea and vanilla soothing my senses. I glanced to my left and noticed a customer at the bookshelf with a book in his hand. Usually at this time of day we had several customers, and a couple of regulars sitting at a table, but the shop was empty and Brenna was not there. This was unusual when there were customers in the store. I walked toward the counter and lifted up a latch. A section of the counter swung open, allowing me to step behind it. I bent over to set my backpack down on a shelf under the counter. When I straightened, I jumped, surprised to find myself nose to nose with the man who had been standing across the store when I entered. He was average looking, with brown hair, and was about six feet tall. He was wearing black slacks and a white button-down shirt, which in itself wasn't that unusual, but he was also wearing a pair of sunglasses and black leather driving gloves. The store was dim from the late afternoon sun, and typical of Southern California weather for October, it was in the mid-eighties outside. The glasses and gloves struck me as slight overkill on trying to look cool, but it was California, I thought.

His nose, being an inch from my own, startled me and I took a step back. Not liking how close he was, I loudly asked if I could help him with anything and he tilted his head slightly to the side and didn't answer. Even though he was wearing dark sunglasses, I felt his gaze run up and down my body, ending on the gold ring on my right hand. The ring started to get that tingling feeling, like it was a battery charging up. I moved my left hand over to touch the ring and twisted it. I asked again, "Sir, is there something I can help you with?" My instincts told me that he wasn't here to buy tea. I backed up a step.

"I am looking for Brenna Cameron, or her niece?" he said making a long hissing sound when he said the word niece. He leaned forward over the counter as he spoke, his breath smelling of sulfur. The counter was about a foot and a half wide, a pretty large barrier between us, but I felt threatened by his intensity. Just as I was about to respond with a sharp rebuke, the chime on the door jingled as the door to the shop opened and Cole stepped inside. He glanced quickly around the store and walked to stand behind the man at the counter.

"Cole! Is it time for us to head to the movie already?" I raised my eyebrows at him and kind of jerked my head towards the man in front of me. I had no idea what Cole was doing here, but I was very glad for the surprise visit and hoped he didn't mind I was using him as an excuse. "I just need to wait until Brenna comes from the back, then I'll be ready to go."

If Cole thought my behavior was weird, he covered his surprise well. "It's cool, we have time." He said looking intently at the man standing in front of me. He moved slightly to the side, removing his hands from the pockets of his sweatshirt and flexing them.

The stranger stepped away from the counter and faced Cole, like two gunslingers in a western movie. He stood with his hands away from his body, and a humming energy filled the air. I saw Cole clench his hands into fists and the ground rumbled. A teapot that was sitting on a burner behind me shrieked, steam rising out of its spout. Scared by the abrupt sound of the teapot, I jumped, and a yellow bolt of energy shot from my hands and hit a bookstand across the shop. Books flew, and a few pages littered the air. I gasped and started to lift my hands, when I noticed the steam from the still shrieking teapot whirl around the stranger's head and neck, turning them red with heat. The man gave Cole and I a calculated glance, turned, and raced from the shop, the bells on the door chiming his exit.

Cole relaxed his hands and went to the door, turning the sign from Open to Closed and locking the door.

"Are you okay? Did he hurt you?" He spoke urgently as he walked quickly towards the counter. Brenna entered the room through the door to the kitchen, wiping her hands on a kitchen towel and Cole and I both jumped. She paused in the doorway, looked at the books littering the floor of the store and at me, pushing my hair out of my face.

"What happened?" she asked in concern.

After I lifted the shrieking teakettle off the burner, I flipped the latch on the counter and stepped towards Cole. "Did you see that? That lightning bolt, or whatever? I think that came from me!" I exclaimed. Since my first day of school, there were little things that I had noticed and tried to overlook about myself and my new friends. Ana's skin changing colors, Summer's speed, Cole making the dust devil on the soccer field, Ben's leaps and grabs in the goal, and the little bursts of power coming from me, or my ring. I grabbed Cole's arm. "And you, too, Cole. The steam from the kettle wrapped around that man and burned him! Did you do that?" I said tightening my grip on his arm. I turned it over, looking at his hand, trying to see if it looked different than my own.

"You... We did this?" I stumbled over words as I tried to figure out how I could have shot that lightning bolt out of my hands.

Brenna looked at Cole and at his nod said, "Come on honey, let's sit down, I think we need to tell you a few things."

"I think so, this is some crazy stuff!" I said rubbing my shaking hands together for warmth. "How is it possible that I have—and Cole has—the power to make things explode, and the steam?"

Brenna explained that there was an entire world of Others. "My family, the Camerons, were witches." At my look of shock, she quickly explained. "Not the witches you see kids dressed up as for Halloween, but Seers and Spell Makers. Powers in our family follow the mother's line and well, we gain them when we turn sixteen."

"Sixteen?" I ask, back to that first day of school and my class appearing to freeze. *Wow*, I thought, *I did that?*

Brenna nods and continues. "Before sixteen, the extent of our powers are a mystery. We have a normal childhood." She stopped when I gave a huff. But when I waved a hand she continued. "On the eve of our sixteenth birthday, at the stroke of midnight, we have our transition, in a kind of trance. It's different for everyone, but when we wake up we have our powers. Some are more powerful than others." Brenna shrugged modestly.

"Like your knowledge of herbs?" I asked.

"Exactly. I'm very happy to create teas that help people feel better. Your mother's talents were in being able to see the truth, a kind of human lie detector. A useful skill, but not too powerful. I think your mother and I were a little bit of a disappointment to the family line. You see, your grandmother, my mother, was one of the strongest Seers the Cameron family had seen in the last century. She had been able to make true predictions of the future."

I remembered how my mother would always know if someone had the money to purchase her survival kits or was trying to take advantage of us. I felt proud that my mom had a useful skill that kept us alive and gave us an income over the last few years, and I said as much to Brenna. She hugged me gently in response.

I turned to Cole and pointed a finger at him. "How do you fit into these Others?" I asked and Cole gave a slight grin.

"I am an Elemental." He said flicking a hand out and sending some loose tea into a small tornado across the table. "Elementals are men who can call on the four elements, Earth, Air, Water, and Fire. As Seers powers are matriarchal, Elementals powers develop only on the male side."

"Do you develop your powers at the same age as, um, Seers?" I stumbled over the unfamiliar name cautiously.

"No, Elemental boys get their power at the age of twelve when the boys um, enter puberty." Cole blushed slightly, the tips of his ears turning pink. I hid a smile looking away. He was so cute!

"Your father, Mathis, is one of the strongest Elementals to be born to his line in the last century. His ability to call on all four elements has given his family tremendous wealth and power. With powers over all four elements, there's not much your father can't do." Cole spoke with a fervor of pride in my father's accomplishments that confused me.

"Have you seen him? My father?" I asked looking hopefully at Cole, and he nodded, glancing down at his clasped hands.

"Your father is friends with Cole's father, honey. Your father arranged for Cole's family to move here a couple of years ago, hoping that you and your mother would someday come through town to see me." Tears filled Brenna's eyes, "But we never expected you to show up on your own."

Remembering what brought me to town, I nodded slowly, then had a thought and looked up at Cole, my eyes narrowed and a ball of hurt filled my chest.

"Is my father still alive?" I asked. When my dad left us, my mother kept saying he had to go away so he could work hard to come back to us. As a little girl, I just couldn't understand why he would choose to leave. Then, when my mom just stopped talking about him and then got more and more paranoid, I tried to ask her about him again but my mother actually cried, trying to explain that he had promised her he'd come back. She seemed so upset that it was just easier to avoid the subject. When I think about how she died trying to sell her survival kits so she and I could eat, it made me sad. But it also made me mad.

I had only a few memories of my father but could only visualize him from a photo I had of him tossing me into the air when I was a baby. I was giggling and my father had a big smile on his face. I wish that photo had been a full shot of him, but it was only a profile. Even so, I could tell that I looked like him, having the same two-toned blonde and brown hair.

Cole answered, "Your father is now the First Sentinel of the Elementals." He said that with pride, his face militaristic. I realized from his reaction that this was a big deal to him.

At my questioning look Brenna explained, "The First Sentinel is the leader of the Elementals. As leader, he sits on the first seat of the Committee, a combined group of

Seers and Elementals who make the decisions and laws for our people. Years ago, the plan was for Mathis to immerse himself back into Elemental society, so that he could provide some sort of protection for you and your mother. Your father has used his abilities over all four elements to gain power and rise through the ranks until he achieved First Sentinel status." I was confused by the sadness in my aunt's voice as she told me this and I looked to Cole for an explanation, but he misinterpreted my look and went on to explain more about Elemental hierarchy.

"When you have powers over several elements, you are considered more valuable to your community. You're given higher levels of training, and if you excel you can become Guardians." Cole's eyes were shining as he spoke.

"Guardians? Of what?" I asked. This was a bit much to take in. My mom and I had been on the run for nine years, but my dad was now the leader of his people? When had that happened? If he was the leader, why had my mom and I moved around constantly? My head was spinning with all of this new information, and I looked back at Cole, trying to focus on what he was saying.

Cole ran his hands through his hair. That, combined with the earlier battle, had given him a cute, rakish, rather disheveled look. His hair stood straight up in the front around his cowlick, and his eyes had turned purple with intensity. "A Guardian is taught to use his powers offensively and defensively, serving the Committee. Your father moved my family to Dover so I could be your Guardian and protect you."

I flashed back to soccer practice when the wind kicked up suddenly, and then here, today, with the ground shaking and the steam burning that man. "But you're the same age I am! How can you protect me?" I asked.

Cole looked embarrassed, but straightened up in his seat and said, "I have been in training to be a Guardian since I gained my powers four years ago."

Brenna jumped in with an explanation, "Cole can use three elements, and because his father and your father are close, and you both are close in age, he was assigned to you." She looked undecided, but continued, "When your mom became pregnant by your father, it was assumed by the Committee that it was you that was prophesied. The first child born from the union of a Seer and an Elemental, since your grandmother's vision."

"Wait." I held up a hand. Jumping up out of my chair to pace in front of the table. "I think you guys skipped a part. Prophecy? Me?" *Information overload*, I thought.

"Your grandmother spoke of a prophecy that said the birth of a daughter with mixed Other blood would cause a power shift, ending the peace that has lasted between our kind for the last two hundred years. Because of this prophecy, the two Elementals and Seers, who had been close allies, separated."

"But you all get along now, right?" I asked.

"Yes, but at first, only the Committee knew about the prophecy. After your parents fell in love the Committee decided it was better for the younger generations to know about it. To keep other people from making the same mistake." Brenna looked sad and distant as she spoke these words but nodded towards Cole. "Cole was taught about the prophecy at a young age." Cole nodded in agreement.

"So, how did my parents meet if Seers and Elementals were forbidden from getting together?"

"I'm afraid it was partly my fault." Brenna said. "Your mother kept me company on my walks in the woods to gather herbs. One day we came across Mathis practicing his craft and the rest was history. They fell instantly in love." She told the story with sadness. "Soon they were meeting in secret, when they became eighteen, they wanted to marry. They told our families and everyone was horrified. They were forbidden to see each other, but they were already pregnant with you." Brenna blinked back tears.

I fought my own tears, realizing now, why my mother and I had been on the run all of those years. "If my father was climbing the ranks in order to change things so that he could help my mother and I why didn't we ever hear from him?" I asked my aunt and her lips tightened in anger.

I had another thought and spoke before she could answer. "I've been here for a couple weeks. Why hasn't he come to see me?" That hazy memory of a father who smiled and swung me around in his arms dimmed and my heart shriveled.

"I wanted to be sure that you were his daughter before I said anything to my father." Cole winced and spoke up quickly, seeing the hurt on my face.

I glanced down at the ring on my right hand and reached over with my left hand to twist it. Cole quickly covered my hand with his and gave it a squeeze. "I don't think you should twist that ring," he said, "it seems to be a focus for whatever powers you're getting." I remembered earlier when I had zapped the bookshelf, and nodded, confused.

"That raises another question." I said trying not to twist my ring. *I really need to find another nervous tic*, I thought crazily, as if that were the least of my problems after hearing about all of this!

"Why do I even have any powers?" I declared, looking back and forth between Brenna and Cole.

"Well, girls aren't supposed to develop their powers until they are sixteen and the fact that yours are materializing early may mean that the prophecy is correct." Brenna spoke with a grim look in her eye. "This could also be why we haven't heard from your father. It could really make things difficult for him as the Sentinel."

Great. I just moved to a new town, found an aunt I didn't know I had, made some friends who just so happen to have some kind of freaky gifts, and found out my father was alive and the leader of the Elementals. I didn't even know Elementals existed, and even more important, he hasn't even come to see me! What else could happen? Oh yeah. "So, who do you think that guy was in the store and what did he want?" I asked, looking at the doorway into the store, as if someone was going to come storming through it.

"I'm not sure," Brenna said, "but, there was a group of both Seers and Elementals who weren't happy about your mom and dad, so he could be from that group."

"Okay, great." I said, thinking that we needed to step up our security on this place if I was going to have this group popping in to do who knows what to me.

Chapter 5

Avery

Ana and I walked out of Biology class, and I looked back with a shudder. We had just finished dissecting a cow eyeball and I could still smell the formaldehyde. Ana, with a skip in her step, was about to walk past Cole who had been leaning up against the wall next to the door. "Hey," he said to us, and we both responded "hi" back. Ana giggling slightly as she gave me a glance and moved to her locker. He walked with us over to the lockers, which were on the same wall only a couple of feet apart. As I turned the combination on mine, he leaned up against it, next to me. I shoved my biology book and iPad into the locker and grabbed my bag lunch and looked over at him.

"What's up?" I asked quietly, trying to be low key. After our discussion yesterday, I felt even more nervous around him than I did before. I mean, here's this guy, who is totally cute, can play Air, Water, and Earth like they're instruments, and who is also my own personal bodyguard? I didn't know how to act around him, but I was determined to not let that nervousness show, so I straightened my spine.

"I thought I'd walk to lunch with you guys," he said, looking down the row of lockers towards Ana. I looked over and saw her grab her lunch bag out of her locker and shut the door. I noticed, once again, that her skin tone had changed colors, making her blend in slightly with the beige wall.

"Sure," I said, and we headed down the hall towards the cafeteria. As we neared the Quad, I saw Summer and Ben sitting under a tree in the shade.

Ben looked up. "Cole!" he yelled. Summer looked at us and waved. We walked past a couple of kids who were throwing a football to each other. As one boy threw to the other, the ball started to sail straight towards Summers head. I started to take a breath to yell at her to look out, when Ben, swiveled his head to the side slightly and leaped straight up from a sitting position, his hand reaching up and scooping the football from in front of her face to his chest. He landed standing up and threw the ball back to the other guy.

"Thanks, sugar," Summer said, reaching her hand out to hold his as he sat back down next to her. Ben grabbed a French fry off her plate and stuck it in his mouth.

Wow, that was an incredible catch! I looked around at my group of friends for a reaction but noticed nobody seemed surprised. Apparently, Cole and I weren't the only ones who had some unique gifts.

Let's just get this out in the open, I thought to myself. "Okay," I said to the group, looking each one of them in the eye. "Is there something you'd all like to share with me?" Yesterday, when Cole and Brenna told me about my background as the daughter of a Seer and Elemental, that I might develop powers, and that Cole, being an Elemental, already had powers, I wondered about some of these unique abilities I kept seeing in my friends. Brenna had mentioned Others but didn't really get past Cole's background and mine.

Cole, knowing what I was going to ask, leaned over to Ben and said with a smirk, "Show her what you can do." Ben looked at me and blinked. His blink was not like my blink, which was normal with one eyelid moving from the top to the bottom of my eye. He had two lids, one that blinked from the top, and one from the bottom of his eye, and met in the center. He looked over at Summer's plate of food and I noticed a French fry fly into his mouth. He chewed slightly and grinned.

"What," I asked, my mouth hanging slightly open, "was that?" Ben's tongue unfurled from his mouth and zipped over to grab another fry from Summer's plate.

"Watch the tongue, Ben!" Summer laughed, biting into her cheeseburger.

"Guys, throw the ball over here again!" Ben called over to the two boys throwing the football. The ball was thrown our way and Ben leaped from a sitting position and scooped the ball up again. This time, he didn't throw it back, but turned his hand over. The ball stuck to his hand.

"Take it from me," Ben said, as he held the ball out towards me. I tried to take it, but it was seriously stuck to his hand! Ben curled his palm in slightly and the ball released from his palm with a small sound and popped into my hand. I stepped towards him and said, "Let me see your hand." He held his hand out and flexed his palm slightly. When he did that, these little suction cups popped out. When he curled his hand in slightly, the suction cups disappeared. He took the ball and threw it back. I looked at him with my mouth hanging open and he reached out and closed it.

"Don't want to catch any flies in there, do you?" His eyes gleamed as he laughed and Cole gave him a high five.

"Stop playing with her," Summer laughed. "Ave, Ben's dad is a frog shifter and his mom is human." She said it so matter of fact, reaching for Ben's hand again and tugging him down next to her. I turned that over in my mind and closed the door on that picture with a shudder.

"You mean, his dad can turn into a frog? Like at the full moon or something? Do you do that too?" I laughed in amazement looking at Summer. Everyone laughed.

"Nah, I don't shift into anything, but I have inherited a little bit of his traits." Ben said nonchalantly. "My dad's family emigrated here from South America a couple of generations ago."

"Where'd that blonde hair come from then?" I asked mockingly, and Ben laughed.

"The California sunshine, babe!"

I laughed and shook my head. Then a thought occurred to me, "Wait a second, you're our goalie, doesn't that give our team an unfair advantage?"

"Nah, Ventura's team has a monkey shifter for a goalie." I looked at him like he was crazy. "No, seriously, sometimes after the game they have a hard time getting him off the goal posts, but he's a great goalie!" Ben laughed as he said it, but his eyes were serious.

I turned to Ana. "Okay, you're next. Don't think I haven't noticed your skin changes color!" I said to her. As we all watched Ana, I noticed that her hand, which was resting on the ground at her side, had turned a slight green tint, blending in with the grass.

Ana smiled with quiet delight, "You're right, I'm a Chameleon." She held up her hand, and I saw little swirls appear on her skin and then separate into groups of freckle clusters. The color of her skin had turned back to a beautiful peachy tint. Her eyes turned a warm shade of brown. Ben let out a soft whistle and Summer slugged him in the arm.

"That explains why no one ever seems to remember you." I said to her, nodding towards Summer and also thinking back to my first day of class when Mr. Newsome argued with her about whether she'd been in class before.

Summer chimed in with, "Sorry about that, Ana!"

"No problem, Summer, my instinct is to always blend in," Ana said quietly, "but I can also change my skin color at will." She put her hand in front of Summer's brown leather purse, and the freckles in her hand swirled and disappeared, her skin tone changing to an almost exact match.

"Okay, so we have Frog boy, a Chameleon, and what are you?" I asked looking directly at Summer. Summer held out her arm and fur started sprouting from the top of it. I really wasn't trying to catch flies, but my mouth was open as I watched her arm grow long golden fur. Her nails were now long claws that looked like they could shred through steel, the tips still painted with red polish. Her nose had flattened slightly and I could see ears peeking through her still long blonde hair.

"I'm a cat shifter." Summer yawned, showing a mouthful of very sharp teeth that hadn't been there a moment ago. "You know the full moon thing is just creative storytelling." She stretched her arm back out, shut her eyes and grimaced. The hair, teeth, and nails receded back into her human form.

"Shifters have lived in this area for a couple generations. Everyone in my family has cat like traits, but my immediate family more closely resembles a mountain lion. Of course, we don't completely shift into a mountain lion. We still walk on two legs."

"But didn't Ana say that you moved here only a few years ago?"

"My father is from this area and went away to college in Georgia. That's where my mom and her family is from." She answered with a thickened southern drawl.

"That does explain your super speed and how athletic you are on the soccer field." I pictured Summer playing soccer with a family of cat shifters. Each one fast and having great foot, hand, and eye coordination. I don't think I'll be joining their pick up games!

"But, isn't it hard to hide what you are from everyone here?" I waved my hand at the other kids throwing the football around and eating lunch. Everyone laughed, and Cole pointed out a girl sitting at the table under the tree close by. She had been talking to a friend and at Cole's whistle her head spun around on her neck, so that it was looking at us, but her body was still facing in the other direction. Her eyes glowed yellow, and then she gave a long slow blink, and her head twisted back around. I gasped, and Cole said, "Ayla is part Owl. Dover is filled with kids who are a little Other."

Knowing that everyone was a little different made me feel less anxious about sharing my story with them. I looked at my friends and started talking.

"Well since you all have been straight with me, I have something to share too." Cole and I took turns re-telling my story and also what happened in the store yesterday. They were already aware of Cole's powers, but were impressed that he had been assigned as my Guardian.

Summer sat up from her lounging position and nodded her head at Cole. "Cool, that he's your Guardian, Aves, but he can't be with you every moment of the day." She looked at Ana, who nodded back at her. "We'll all keep an eye out and help when Cole's not around." Ben nodded and slung his arm around Summers shoulders giving her hair a tug in approval.

Ana, who had been quiet up to that point, asked the question: "So, this guy in the store belongs to some group that wants to hurt you?"

"Well, we don't really know." I answered, looking at Cole to see if he had any information to add. During our conversation, I had noticed that Cole, even as he contributed to the discussion, was scanning the area. He normally had his hands in the pockets of his hoodie—todays hoodie was red and black with the school's logo over the chest—but his hands were out of his pockets, in preparation for action, I guess. I glanced around but didn't see anything out of the ordinary. *Well, more extraordinary, anyway*, I thought.

Cole gave the group a serious look. "I think we can expect trouble. Avery's powers are supposed to kick in on her birthday." He looked at me in question.

"In two weeks," I said, "on Halloween."

Ana gasped, her freckles whirling madly, and her skin changed to the color of the tree's bark that she was leaning against. "Samhain!"

Summer looked at her curiously, "I'm not liking the sound of that gasp, Sugar. Why don't you fill us in?"

Cole spoke before Ana could, "it's the longest day of the year, and the one day of the year that the veil between our world and another is really thin." Ana nodded in agreement. "But in addition to that, legend has it that a couple hundred years ago a pair of evil Other Spell Casters named Atticus and Gaea cast a spell at 12:01 a.m. on Samhain, trying to bring forth the Daïmon Avdar into our dimension. No one knows why they were trying to summon him, but when they did, they were not able to hold him and he escaped into our world."

"Dude, what happened to him?" Ben asked, his horrified look interrupted by one of Summers french fries flying into his mouth.

"Well, if that legend is true, then he is still loose in our world. When he was summoned, they stole his power." Cole shrugged and stretched the fingers of his hands out, knuckles lightly popping. "No one has seen him since. But you guys, there is a second part to the prophecy. Remember the first part says that the child from the union of a Seer and Elemental will have tremendous power unheard of before, but the second part said that that child would have the power to vanquish the Daïmon Avdar."

Surprised, I looked around at my friends, wondering, just as they were, I'm sure, if I was actually that person. I mean, I didn't feel like I had some kind of incredible power that could strike against a Daïmon. *I hope I'm not this prophesied person*, I thought to myself, *because if I am, I need to up my game. A lot!*

I ran backwards keeping pace with the girl dribbling the ball towards me. Out of the corner of my eye, I could see another girl wearing a blue jersey moving into an open space between two of our defenders. As her leg went back for the kick to her teammate, I changed direction, moving forward and into the lane to intercept her pass. Running forward, I tapped the ball with the outside of my foot, ran around a blue jersey, and glanced across the field looking for red and black jerseys. Summer was being covered by two players, but I knew she'd free herself up for the pass. The girl defending my advance was the same girl I had just stripped the ball from the moment before and saw she was looking at me in intense concentration, like she had something to prove. As my toe hit the ball to send a pass across the field to Summer, the other player slid through the grass in a tackle that should've taken me down, but without a thought, I gestured towards her and her slide stopped abruptly, like she had hit a wall. Her body crumpled up into a standing position, with her face pressed to the side against that invisible wall, and then falling backwards into a heap on the ground. As I stood there, pins and needles gathered in my hand and then dissipated. I looked at my hand and shook it out, wondering if I'd had anything to do with that move. I heard my teammates yelling, Summer had just put us in the lead, taking my pass, and with one tap placing it in the goal.

The player on the ground stirred and looked over at a spot on the ground, and I looked too! We were both searching for the reason that her tackle stopped abruptly. That could NOT have been me, could it? I looked at my hand in horror. It seemed the same. I looked back at the player and noticed that she had shrugged it off and was limping over to the sideline, where she was subbed out of the game.

I ran over to Summer to congratulate her and saw Cole, Ben, and Ana standing on the sidelines. They were wearing their black and red jerseys, as the boys' varsity team had played the game before ours. I saw Cole was staring at the spot on the other side of the field, but Ben, as if he knew I had created that invisible wall, was looking directly at me and smiled, "That was lit, Avery!" I looked at my hand, caught his wink and waved it at him, with a smirk on my face.

As Summer and I approached the side of the soccer field, the referee blew his whistle, signaling the end of the game. Cole, Ben, and Ana congratulated us with pats on the back. As we headed towards the locker room, Cole asked if we all wanted to meet up at Gino's Pizza to celebrate.

"I could use a slice," Summer said, and I agreed, my stomach rumbling at the thought. We had gotten into the habit over the last couple of weeks to go for pizza after a game. Summer was always starving and could usually finish a Meat Lovers pizza by herself. The first time I had seen her finish one off, I went home feeling a little ill. Now, it just seemed normal. Really weird, but for Summer, normal. We all agreed to meet up at Gino's and Summer and I walked off towards the locker room.

As the two of us entered the locker room, I glanced up at a sign posted to the wall inside the door. Dover High Sadie Hawkins Dance, it read. The sign had a couple dressed up in Elvis and Priscilla Presley costumes, dancing under a full moon. There were jack-o-lanterns decorating each corner of the poster, and there was the image of a witch on a broomstick flying across the front of the moon. "Are you and Ben going to the Dance?" I asked Summer, nodding towards the sign as we passed it. This year the dance fell on October 30 and was being treated as more of a Halloween party, but the tradition of the girl asking the boy still applied.

"I asked him today at lunch and he said he'd like to go. He mentioned doubling with you and Cole. What do you think?" She laughingly looked my way. Ana, Summer, and I had gone shopping the other day and I had fished around for information on Cole. I thought I'd been pretty casual about it, but apparently I hadn't been casual enough.

I shrugged, feeling that awkward flush head up my neck again. I wasn't sure how I felt about asking him to the dance and said as much to Summer. I thought initially there had been a little bit of chemistry between Cole and me, but since his Guardian secret was out, I wasn't sure if hanging out with me wasn't just a job.

"I'm not sure I should," I answered. "Maybe he's not allowed. I mean, it's not like he's hanging out with me because he likes me. He kind of has to, you know?" I pulled my towel out of my locker and started going through my gym bag looking for my clean clothes.

"Ben wouldn't have suggested it if he'd thought Cole wouldn't go for it. I know Cole takes this Guardian job seriously, but I think there's more to him than just that. Since I've known him, he's never shown any interest in a girl, and he's had plenty of chances." Summer grabbed her entire bag and headed towards the shower but threw a comment over her shoulder on the way out of the room, "You'll never know unless you ask him!" *True*, I thought. My stomach rumbled with hunger, but it was now accompanied by a burn of panic.

Chapter 6

Cole

As I ran down the field, keeping an eye on Eric, a teammate with the ball at midfield, I felt the air currents change. The grass was whispering to me that someone was tracking my steps. Ahead, Eric looked to his right and left, trapped by two opponents. I flicked my fingers out slightly and a chunk of dirt exploded out of the ground in front of one of his opponents, surprising him slightly so that he mis-stepped, creating an opening that Eric passed the ball through. Hearing a breath, I tapped the ball to the left and spun after it, turning to view the player behind me. He was three steps back and I recognized that he was drawing power. I had just enough time to maneuver away and swing my leg back giving a solid kick to the ball before he could strike, delivering it neatly beyond their goalkeeper's fingertips and swooshing against the back of the net. Goal!

I grinned wildly, teeth clenched in triumph, turned, and headed back to midfield, bumping chests with Eric, who had run over to celebrate our goal. I glanced back at Ben, who was yelling wildly for the defense to set up. Our coach was yelling that there were only a couple of seconds left in the game. The other team raced with the ball to midfield, trying to get the game started and catch us off guard. They tapped the ball forward and the referee blew the whistle three times signaling the end of the game. I heard the crowd yelling and the members of our team calling out to each other to celebrate our win.

"Awesome!" Ben flung an arm over my shoulder. "That kick soared, dude!"

I grinned and shrugged his arm off my shoulder. "Come on let's check out how the girls' game is going." We shook the hand of the other team goalie and headed over to our bags on the side of the field. Ben grabbed his things as well and we started walking over to the field adjacent to ours.

As we walked, I pulled the barbell, usually attached to my eyebrow, out of the side pocket of my bag and hooked it back into my piercing, as it connected it gave my skin a little jolt. Ben laughed, "Coach should just let you keep it in."

"Nah, it's cool." I said. Coach was a stickler for not having any kind of jewelry on the field, giving an opponent an opportunity to grab onto something. A lot of the guys had earrings or nose piercings that they had to take out before the game.

As we got near the girls' game, I could see Ana standing on the sidelines, her hands gripped in front of her. Ben and I walked up and joined her just as Avery came dribbling the ball up the sideline.

"Uh-oh, she's going to get squashed!" Ana whispered to Ben, her freckles swirling in agitation. The opponent started her slide tackle and Avery flicked out a hand and the girl, well, just stopped! Recognizing that she used Air to create a shield, I stared in surprise. Avery looked surprised at what she'd done, but still drilled the ball towards Summer, who took it down the field for a goal.

"Awesome!" Ben and I yelled and clapped each other on the back. Ana quietly smiled and clapped her hands together. A few minutes later the game ended, with our school getting the win. Summer and Ana walked towards us and Ben spoke first, "Cool play, Avery!"

I noticed a couple of girls from the other team helping their teammate walk off the field toward the parking lot, one of them speaking to a dark-haired man in a white button-down shirt and black sunglasses. His head turned in our direction and we made eye contact. He turned his head and looked down the sideline and I followed his gaze.

"What the hell?" I nudged Ben and jerked my head towards the other side of the field. There was a group of men, all dressed similarly in white button-downs, dark slacks, sunglasses, and gloves spaced about three feet apart from each other staring across the field at us. Ana, Summer, and Avery were already heading to the locker room to change clothes so they could meet us out for pizza.

"Bruh, this is weird. What do you think that's all about?" Ben flanked my left side.

"I'm not sure, but I think we should find out." I said. Feeling the energy start to course through my hands as I gathered it from the Earth. We walked across the field most of the players, their friends, and families had already started to head toward either the parking lot or the locker room, so it was Ben and me and those six men.

One of them stepped forward, and then suddenly the other five were arranged behind him in pyramid formation. As they stood next to each other, I realized that not only were they dressed similarly, but they all looked exactly alike. I stepped forward to meet the man in front, my hands loose at my sides. The wind picked up slightly.

As I got closer, the man in the lead shook his arms and flexed his hands. I stopped Ben, worried for his safety.

"Why don't you wait here? I'm going to see what he wants."

"Man, this doesn't look like it's going to be friendly. All the same to you, I'm coming too." Ben's skin started to take on a green sheen, emitting a wet fragrance, and as he took a large breath of air his body started expanding and growing bigger. I stepped away from him slightly. I didn't want to touch his skin, even by accident. Ben's touch would numb that area, making it impossible to move even a finger. He was my friend, but I knew his instinctive reaction to a predator was to use his best defense, his toxic skin. Friend or no, if he touched me, it would not be good. His tongue flicked out and grabbed the glasses off one of the guys to the right, flinging them to the ground. The man blinked and his eyes glowed red.

"Shit. Daïmonids." I said to Ben, a chill running up my back. Mentally, I ran through some of my training. I curled a finger and started a whirlwind to the right of the lead Daïmonid, holding it steady in place. Daïmonids were used primarily for small disturbances and skirmishes. Even though they were lower class, they were still really dangerous. We needed to get a handle on this and quick!

Fire shot out of the Daïmonid's red eyes, burning a line along the ground towards Ben. Ben bent his knees and leaped over the Daïmonid and its fire line. Coming up behind him, he grabbed him around the neck, making the Daïmonid shriek with pain. It popped, disappearing, and leaving a dark streak on the ground and scorching Ben's jersey and shorts, with smoke lingering behind.

I focused my attention on the leader. "What do you want?" I said. No answer, instead the Daïmonid launched himself towards me. I flung my arm, hitting him solidly in the side with the whirlwind, sending energy and wind into it so that it took on greater size, ripping out pieces of earth and flinging them into the face of the Daïmonid.

"No small talk? All right, let's do it!" I grimaced feeling the force of my power. I noticed one of the Daïmonids trying to circle around my back and I turned slightly to the right, keeping my whirlwind in sight, using it to hit the other Daïmonid, and eyeing the new one. I reached up and touched the barbell in my eye, giving my body a jolt, then pointed at the Daïmonid, a purple bolt of electricity arcing from my finger directly into his chest. The Daïmonid exploded and black smoke curled up from the ground.

I could hear Ben engaging with one of the other Daïmonids, taunting him and spitting into its face. The spit spattered as it landed, and the Daïmonid's yell was interrupted when its body disintegrated. I paused in admiration. Venom? I hadn't a clue that Ben had anything other than strength, agility and toxic skin. *I'm glad he's on my side*, I thought, as I focused my gaze on the leader.

He was struggling against the wind and debris, so I thought quickly. We were now 3 to 2. Not horrible odds. Ben seemed to be holding his own even though he wasn't trained for this type of battle, and I wanted to quickly end it. I arched my back, splaying my arms out to my sides while my power sizzled within me, looking at the sky, I gave a yell and flung my hand down ripping the ground open under our enemy. Two of them fell into the earth, leaving only the leader to face me down.

"Back where you belong, Daïmonid!" I snarled in the leader's face and focused my mind towards a sprinkler on the right. Remembering from my training that they could be destroyed by water. I sent the wind into the earth to rip it free and wrapped the pipe around the leader, slowly pushing him back toward the gaping chasm with the force of my wind. Small cuts from flying grass littered his face, as he shoved against my power. Water was shooting into the air where the sprinkler had come free, the spray dampening the streaks of fire scorched into the soccer field and sizzling on the Daïmonids skin.

"The prophecy will not come true!" the Daïmonid screamed at me as my wind storm pushed him into the earth. I clapped my hands and the ground moved back together, making what looked to be a grave over where the Daïmonids had entered the earth.

I pushed my now-wet hair off my forehead and checked out my hands for any cuts that needed tending. *Not too bad*, I thought. Looking over at Ben who was now shrinking back towards his normal size and the green cast to his skin was starting to fade. "Thanks, Ben, for watching my back," I said, turning towards him and after another glance at his color, flinging my arm around his shoulders. I gave him a quick squeeze. "So, you said your dad's family was from South America?" At his nod, I continued. "Dart frog, right?"

Ben grinned and answered, "Yeah."

I looked around in regret at the mess we'd made of the soccer field. "You still up for pizza?" I waved a hand out and sent power to smooth out the field, pushing a little energy into the earth making the grass grow an inch. All signs of our battle gone.

"Absolutely!" He grinned and flicked a tongue out, snatching a bug out of the air in front of him and yanking it into his mouth. "I'm starving!" We turned around and walked towards the locker room, Ben chewing slightly. "You are eventually going to tell me what's going on, aren't you?" Ben asked.

"Yeah, as soon as I figure it out myself," I replied back.

Chapter 7

Avery

As we entered Gino's, I spotted our friends at a booth in the corner where Cole was pouring some soda from a pitcher into several glasses on the table. As we walked towards them, people reached out to pat Summer and me, calling out "Good game!" I felt a flush of pleasure as I followed Summer as she strolled through the tables smiling at everyone, her blonde hair glinting in the lights. We turned down several invitations to sit with teammates and headed toward the back booth. All of this attention made me a little uncomfortable but it was nice to belong. I waved at a couple of our teammates sitting across the room. Summer ate it up.

Ana and Ben were sharing one side of our table and Cole sat alone on the other side. Summer, giving me a sly look, sat on the end next to Ben, leaving the empty seat next to Cole open. He stood up as I started to sit and motioned me to scoot over towards the wall. He sat down next to me and put his arm on the edge of the booth behind me. *The better to guard me*, I thought.

Ben, Summer, and Ana started talking, re-capping some of the highlights from our game. I listened in and laughed at one of Ben's comments, but then I noticed Cole scanning the restaurant again.

"You can relax, you know. I'm sure this place is too crowded for anything weird to happen." I looked around at the all of the full tables.

"You're probably right." He turned his body to the side to face me a little bit more. His hair was, once again, sticking up in front. The lamp over our table glinted off the silver brow piercing. I looked at my hands, my stomach fluttering. He reached out with the hand that was lying along the back of the booth and pulled on a piece of my hair. That tug startled me into looking up and our eyes caught and held and the fluttering stopped. The corner of his mouth quirked up into a slight smile.

Summer and Ana laughing caught my attention and I looked across the table at Ben waving his hands around while he told a story.

"Summer told me that she and Ben were going to the dance together." I twisted the ring on my right hand. "I know you're stuck doing this Guardian thing, but would you want to go with me?" I asked the question really fast. I had never been to a school dance before, and it probably shouldn't matter so much but I really wanted him to say yes.

Cole reached over and laid his hand over mine to stop the twisting. "That sounds like fun," he said. I looked up at him, a soft buzz of pleasure filled my head and smiled as two pizzas were placed on the table in front of us. I looked over at Summer and she gave me a wink.

"Ana, are you going to the dance?" I reached for a piece of pepperoni pizza.

"I'm on the decorating committee and will be working the refreshment table," she said as she took a bite of her piece.

"Well, you can hang out with us, we're all going together." Summer said as she looked at Ben. She took a bite out of the slice she held in her hand and Ben's tongue nabbed a piece of pepperoni right before it went into her mouth. She smiled and blew him a kiss.

Chapter 8

Cole

I parked my car at the curb in front of my house, turned the car off and reached for the door handle, but before pulling it, I dropped my hand back in my lap. I stared forward out the windshield and thought about the conversation I needed to have with my dad. I knew why we were living in Dover, but after three years, I hadn't thought that the Sentinel's daughter was ever going to show up. I entered school, made friends, and had a more normal life than I'd ever had up to this point. My dad, on the other hand, had to take a more minor role on the committee after moving away. Although my dad and Mathis were still close, my dad seemed disillusioned with our mission. His friend, who had at one time been troubled, asking for his help and advice, was now the Sentinel, the most powerful committee member, and I think my father had come to resent that a little bit.

The front porch light clicked on, jarring me out of my thoughts. I took a steadying breath. I needed to get inside and have that talk with my father. My stomach was tied in knots as I thought of how Avery had asked me to the Sadie Hawkins dance tonight. Man, she was sweet! There was no way this girl had an evil bone in her body. With that thought filling me with purpose I took a breath and reached again for the door handle.

As soon as I opened the front door, my dad looked up from his computer at his desk, the light from the screen creating dark shadows and making a horror mask of my father's face. I threw my backpack on a chair and approached him.

"Dad, can we talk for a second?" I put my hands into the pocket of my hoodie to keep me from nervously clenching them into fists.

"What's up?" My father reached out and turned off the computer, the light dimming until I could see his features more clearly, the mask removed.

I cleared my throat. "So, you know this new girl started at school a couple of weeks ago, Avery Anderson."

My father sat up straighter in his chair, "You texted me the day she started, I've been waiting for your report." He spat the words out and frowned at me. "Why have you taken so long?"

"I wanted to be sure, Dad. She is definitely Sentinel Mathis's daughter, but Dad, I don't think she's power hungry or anything!" I rushed through the words. I needed to convince my father that she was not a threat.

"Have you befriended her?"

"Yes, of course. On her first day." I spoke, a strength to my words, wanting to assure him that I was doing what I was assigned.

My father got up from his seat and walked toward me. "Son, you knew this might be a tough assignment. We need to determine if she will develop these powers."

"Well, her birthday is on Halloween, but she's already done a few things that I think are pretty telling." Standing at attention I proceeded to describe the glowing lights on her first day, her ring, and the wall she threw up in the soccer game that day.

“This is incredible! I need to call Mathis and fill him in,” he exclaimed, starting to hurry from the room.

“Dad, wait! That’s not all that’s happening!” I quickly told him about the Daïmonids attacking Ben and me at the soccer field, and what the leader said about the prophecy not coming true. “You need to let Mathis know that Daïmonids are going to try to kill her!”

My father slowly sank into one of the chairs and rubbed a hand across his mouth.

“This will change everything, Cole.” He looked up at me, his deep blue eyes dark with worry. ”If Avdar is aware that she’s already gained some powers, and it’s not even her sixteenth birthday, she may really be in danger.” He dug his cell phone out of his pocket and walked out of the room. I could hear the murmur of his voice drifting down the hall as he walked away.

“Crap, that’s what I thought too.” Letting the training kick in I organized my thoughts, trying not to let worry creep into my voice. I reached into my pocket for my own cell phone and put a call in to Ben.

“Ben, we need to meet after school at Avery’s house tomorrow. Can you get Summer and Ana to come also? I think we need to start working with Avery, honing her skills so she can defend herself. I’m going to talk to my dad about some training for her.” I said firmly.

Chapter 9

Avery

I was standing behind the counter at the front of the shop when the door chimed, indicating someone had opened the door. *My friends arrived early*, I thought. I looked up, but the sun shining through the front window cast them in shadow, and I couldn't tell who had entered the store. When the sun went behind a cloud, I saw it was Cole and an older man who must be his father who had entered the store. Glancing between the two of them, I could see there was a strong resemblance. Cole's father also had dark hair, though his was cut very short. When he looked my way, I could see that his eyes were a dark shade of blue, not purple like Cole's, and he had smile lines at the corners of his eyes

"Avery, this is my father, Will." Cole looked back at the door as it chimed and nodded at Summer and Ben who walked in together.

"It's nice to meet you Mr. Sullivan." I said, reaching out to shake his hand. This is the man who's friends with my father? He had a nice smile, but as we shook hands I could see a shadow of sadness cross into his eyes, which given the circumstances I thought weird. I looked at Cole, but he was acting his normal positive Guardian self, so I shrugged it off.

"I've told my father about some of the things that have been happening and I thought he could help us evaluate exactly what powers you have already developed. He agrees that we should train you on how to defend yourself." Cole stated and his dad nodded in agreement.

"Brenna has also called me, expressing her concerns," Mr. Sullivan said, looking at my aunt who had just come in from our apartment and nodding a hello. "Is there somewhere we can do a few tests?"

"Why don't you all head out to the back yard? I'll just close the shop and join you." Brenna headed toward the front door, and I led the way into the backyard, my friends and Mr. Sullivan following close behind me.

Brenna's backyard had a small, whitewashed wooden deck overlooking her garden, with flowering pots on either side of the back door. The garden was filled with the aroma of peppermint, verbena, and lavender. Brenna grew her own herbs to use in her special tea mixes. On the deck was a rattan patio set including a table and four cushioned chairs. I took a seat in one of the chairs, and then realized that we didn't have enough seats for everyone. Just as I was getting up, Brenna opened the back door and carried two of the dinette chairs from the kitchen onto the deck. She set them around the table and we scooted our seats over to make room. As everyone was getting comfortable, I noticed a black bird sitting on a branch overhanging the porch. The bird cocked its head to one side and looked directly at me. Brenna, who had gone back inside for refreshments and the lemon bars she had plated earlier, returned to the patio. She set everything on the table and raised her hand slightly. The bird flew down from the branch and landed on her finger. I remembered when I first arrived in Dover and had met Brenna for the first time. I had just told her about my mother dying and she went outside to read the letter my mother had left for her. Her sadness as she wiped tears from her eyes, but also I remembered the blackbird. A ray of sunshine had broken through the clouds and she had turned her face up into the light, flyaway pieces of hair moving lightly around her head, shining in the breeze. Just as she did a moment ago, she raised a finger to the sky and a blackbird flew down from the tree behind her and landed on her finger. It stretched its wings, showing off the red stripe on each wing. She spoke to it, and I swear the bird was listening. It cocked its head and looked straight at Brenna. It seemed to nod, then flew off. Amazed, I looked at my aunt, wondering if this was that same blackbird, and was she communicating with it?

Brenna set the bird down on the edge of the table and reached for the pitcher of tea and started pouring it into glasses, completely ignoring her interaction with the black bird. Summer and I looked at each other, and I shrugged totally not know what had just happened. It certainly wasn't the weirdest thing that had happened since I moved to Dover, but it was the weirdest with my aunt.

"Avery, let's move down into the yard and we'll do a couple tests." Mr. Sullivan's raised voice made me jump out of my chair. Cole also got up from the table as if to join me and his father turned to him and raised an eyebrow. *Now I knew where Cole got that look from*, I thought with an inward grin.

"Cole, you don't need to worry, we are just going to start with a simple test. I'm not going to hurt Avery." Cole slowly sat back down into his chair his face calm, which gave me confidence as I turned to face his father.

"Avery, Cole has told me about your power manifesting early," he looked at me for confirmation, and I nodded confidently. Even though it may not be a good thing, I liked the fact that the power gave me strength. Running with my mom for so long made me feel so helpless. Mr. Sullivan gave me a searching look and continued.

“It’s very important for an Elemental to receive training immediately upon gaining powers, so I need to determine what you can do. Cole tells me that you have an affinity for air?” He asked rather incredulously.

I thought back to the soccer game and how I had stopped that slide tackle with a wave of my hand. I nodded at Mr. Sullivan. “Yes, I think so, but I only called upon Air by accident.” I said in my own defense.

“That’s precisely why we want to test you right now,” he said, speaking firmly but not in an unfriendly way.

I followed Mr. Sullivan down onto the lawn. “Have you ever done any meditation?” He asked, and I shook my head.

“I don’t think so.” I replied. He directed me to stand with my eyes closed and my hands loose at my side. He explained that this was a sort of meditation. I needed to block out my aunt and friends talking quietly at the table behind me, and to focus on the sound of the wind moving through the trees, the birds chirping, the soft sound of a door closing on the street beyond the house.

I closed my eyes and took a deep breath. As I did, I noticed a pinpoint of light forming behind my eyelids. As I concentrated on that light, it expanded until my mind was filled with a warm golden light. I heard a soft flutter by my right ear and the bushes move softly next to me.

“Now, as you breathe out, turn your energy outward.” When he said this, I concentrated on pushing the light within me. There was an energy build up and then a sudden release as the light seemed to move beyond me. I could feel the warmth from it, but it was no longer encompassing my mind.

"Avery, open your eyes and tell me what you see." I slowly opened them and looked around me. In vivid detail I could see every stalk of grass beneath my feet, and its grassy scent mingled with the lavender growing from the bush next to me smelled crisp and strong. I heard three small snips and noticed three golden brown leaves falling gently from the tree overhead. The black bird that had been on the table when I walked down onto the grass was now hovering in the air in front of me. I could hear the sound of its wings fluttering gently. I lifted up my hand to reach a finger out towards the bird, but when I caught sight of my hand I stopped, shocked by its appearance. My hand looked luminescent, casting a golden glow onto the bird in front of me. The bird fluttered its wings as if in a birdbath, washing itself in my energy.

"My hand is glowing!" I exclaimed in astonishment. I watched the bird fly back to my aunt at the table. Its wings were shining with an iridescent light. It tweeted at her and cocked its head and continued to watch.

"Actually, your entire body is glowing." Cole said and I looked toward Mr. Sullivan and saw that Cole had joined him on the grass. "That is your power manifesting," he continued. Cole had taken off his hoodie and he had on a plain white t-shirt and a pair of jeans. I absently noted that this was the first time I had seen him out of a sweatshirt and that he looked totally cute. He was smiling slightly as he reached his hand out towards me.

"Now reach your energy out towards Cole." Mr. Sullivan took a step back from Cole as if to get out of the way.

"I don't want to hurt him!" But my hand was already shifting towards Cole, the sunlight glinting off the gold ring on my right hand, and my energy engulfed him. I felt an arc of energy pulse from me towards him until he was surrounded by a warm glow, just like the first day we met. At the same time, his energy pushed towards me, a slightly cooler essence with a purple hue, surrounding mine until our energies joined together. I felt his cool strength as the space between us was lit with my soft golden light and Cole's light purple light. Cole took a deep breath and let it out gently. A cool breeze intertwined with our combined energies, very intimate, kind of like firelight heating a small cool room. The glowing light started to pulse slightly down through my stomach and I panicked, mentally cutting the cord. Our energy felt like it had fused together, and that pulse–well, I'm not sure what that was, but it made me curious and I looked up slightly embarrassed, then back down when I saw the smirk on his face. I could feel the heat of a blush and hoped he didn't notice.

Mr. Sullivan cleared his throat and looked down at the ground, smiling slightly. "Well, you have definitely started developing."

I heard Brenna and Summer giggle. Sheesh, he didn't need to make it sound like I was going through puberty or something. "Okay, ha ha. I thought you were going to teach me some defensive moves?" I narrowed my eyes at Summer and she raised her hands in front of her laughing.

"Aves, that was hot!" she said, giggling lightly. She reached out for Ben's hand and I watched jealously as they intertwined fingers.

"Yes, okay." Mr. Sullivan moved his gaze from me to Cole, asking Cole to move about five yards away so they could demonstrate an energy attack. The two of them faced each other and Cole flicked his hand out to his side. As he did, a bolt of purple energy shot out towards his father, who lifted his own hand up, fingers spread, and created a shield that the bolt hit, fizzled, and died out on.

Ben called out excitedly from the chair behind me. "Avery you created a shield already, didn't you? On the soccer field."

Cole nodded, "I remember you doing that during the game when that girl was trying to slide tackle you." He looked at his father. "Remember I told you she created a shield instinctively, without any training?" He sounded concerned, and his dad looked at me with a slight frown between his brows, nodding his head in response.

"Well, I guess we'd better get started giving her some." The rest of the afternoon was spent teaching me how to throw bolts of energy and capture them with my shield. According to Mr. Sullivan, I was a quick study and my body hummed its pleasure at learning this art but I learned that even though I seemed to have an affinity for it, my body tired out easily. *I'm going to have to build up a tolerance to this energy*, I thought.

I tried to find the perfect time to ask Mr. Sullivan about my father, but he never let up! I was so disappointed. I wanted to know if my dad knew I was here. If he was going to come see me, but it was like Mr. Sullivan knew I was going to ask and he made sure I was always working with Cole. As the afternoon wore on and my Elemental powers although newly discovered, became a little bit stronger, he got more distant.

I wondered if the same thoughts were running through his head that were going through my own. If I could do all of these things before my sixteenth birthday, what powers would I gain when I actually turned sixteen?

Chapter 10

Cole

The first time I took my dad over to Avery's house, he concentrated on defensive moves. Surprisingly, she could also blast with energy, but I think her real strength may be in her ability to talk to and move the earth. That's why I was headed to her house today to test her affinity with earth.

We both agreed that we would continue training every day after school that we didn't have soccer practice. My dad has created a training regime for me to follow, and trusted me to continue her training myself, which was cool, considering his concern about how powerful she might be. I was just glad to get to spend a little time alone with her. The more I learned about her the better I liked her.

I went around to the side door when I got to her house and gave a quiet knock.

"Hi," she said, as she opened the door. The smell of cornbread swept past her in a rush of warm air, and she brushed a strand of hair behind her ear, moving sideways to allow me room to come in. She quickly looked away from my gaze as I passed by her purposely brushing my shoulder against her arm.

"Hey." I thought it was cute that she still looked shy when she saw me. "What smells so great?" I looked around the room, and said hi to Brenna, who was standing at the stove stirring a spoon around a pot. She raised a brow at me and I felt my face warm as I realized she saw me intentionally brush up against Avery.

"I have been dying to cook a pot of chili now that the weather has gotten a bit cooler." Brenna fought a smile and grabbed a potholder off the counter. She reached into the oven and pulled out a muffin pan.

I glanced at Avery. "Cornbread." Avery said, smiling as my eyes lit up. "You can stay for dinner if you want?" She ended her sentence with a question in her voice. My stomach grumbled in response and I winced slightly with embarrassment, but she laughed

"Awesome." My dad and I did okay with meals, but our skills in the kitchen were limited, we ate sandwiches or ordered in a lot. "Should we go outside to practice?" I glanced out the doors and saw that the sun was still peeking over the trees.

"Yes, go on you two." Brenna waved us outside, and Avery gave me an "after you" sweep of her arm.

"So, what's on the agenda for today's training?" Avery walked over and stood on the lawn, watching me walk towards her.

"Well, the other day with my dad, you were able to draw a shield and send energy towards me. I'd like to see how much ability you have to talk to the earth." I sat down in front of her and patted the ground in front of me. Avery dropped down and sat cross-legged, a perplexed look on her face.

"Do you want me to meditate?" She tilted her head slightly to the right side and sat up a little straighter.

"Well, kind of, but I want you to put your hands down on the grass on either side of you. Concentrate on the feel of it. Picture the grass in your mind." As I spoke, Avery closed her eyes, laying her palms flat on the ground. "Take a deep breath and smell the air." She inhaled deeply and I copied her movements, feeling the buzz of Earth's power channel through me.

"I want you to feel each blade of grass and in your mind, visualize the roots. With your mind only, pull a chunk of the grass out of the ground and float it in front of us." She opened one eye and gave me a look that said I was crazy. I chuckled. "No really, close your eyes. Clear your mind and focus on the feel, smell and energy that is emitting from the grass beneath you. I'll do it with you." I closed my own eyes and lay my palms flat on the ground. The grass pricked my palms, but beneath that touch, I could feel the energy emanating from it.

"Now, focus your energy down into your hands, and pull upwards on the grass with your mind." I envisioned the roots of the grass breaking, and a chunk of earth floating in front of me. I opened my eyes, looking at Avery, and smiled. In front of me was the chunk of grass that I had envisioned. I looked around, and then looked down, then quickly up again in astonishment.

"Ah, Avery? Slowly open your eyes and look around." She had such a peaceful look on her face as she opened her eyes, which quickly faded to panic. We were still sitting on the grass, with my small chunk of earth floating in front of us. Avery, however, had not lifted a small chunk of earth; she had lifted the entire lawn. We were now sitting in her back yard, five feet in the air, on her back lawn.

I opened my mouth to say "Careful," when we dropped abruptly, with an audible thud, back down to the ground.

My teeth clacked together as we hit. I heard the back door open.

"You need to move it slightly to the left, Avery. It's off center now." Brenna said loudly, with a laugh in her voice. Then the door closed and she went back into the house. I looked at Avery and fell backwards, laughing. Her eyes had gone wide in astonishment, but she quickly joined me.

"You're going to have to help me shift the lawn back," she said, giggling.

The next day I picked Avery up on my way in to school and as she sat beside me in my car I tried to think of something to say. I still hadn't told her about the Daïmonids attacking Ben and me at school the other day. I wanted her to get a little more comfortable controlling her powers before I let her know how much danger she was in. I'd been hoping that my father would have more instructions after talking to Mathis, but they were pretty much the same, although my father was acting weird and really stressed out. My orders were still to stay close to Avery, evaluate her powers and protect her. My father, after meeting Avery the other day, was convinced that Avery was the child from the prophecy, but I was holding out hope that it wouldn't be true. The fact that Daïmonids were trying to kill her did seem to point in that direction though. Of course, all of these thoughts weren't helping me come up with something to say.

I opened my mouth to finally speak just as we pulled into the lot, I saw Ben and Summer getting out of his truck. I went around to open Avery's car door, and when she thanked me quietly, I just grinned back at her. *So much for conversation*, I thought. Ben and Summer spotted us and moved in our direction. "Dude." Ben grinned at me.

I saw Summer greet Avery with a "Hey, Ave!" and they started walking across the parking lot towards the school entrance. I saw Avery look to the right, and Ana shifted away from a car she was leaning against. The freckles on her skin swirled, her skin tone changing from the beige of the car she was leaning against to her natural peach tint. Summer jumped when Ana appeared on her left.

"Damn Sugar, you scared me!" Summer bumped shoulders with Ana and giggled.

"Sorry. I saw you guys and thought I'd wait until you caught up." Ana glanced over her shoulder at Ben and me. "Hi Ben, Cole." Still smiling she turned back to the girls. She whispered something to them and they all laughed and kept walking.

As Ben and I stepped up onto the sidewalk, a car pulled into the parking lot, music blaring. Catching my attention, I looked over but I didn't recognize the car, a dark green Camaro. It pulled into one of the teacher's spaces up front and the engine turned off, silencing the music.

"Ben, why don't you take the girls to their lockers. I'm going to check this out for a minute." Ben nodded his head, caught up to Summer, and slung his arm over her shoulder.

"Ladies, let's move this party inside." He bent to Summer's ear and whispered something that made her giggle.

"Come on Aves, Ana. We don't want to be late for homeroom."

Avery glanced over her shoulder at me, but I was too busy checking out the guy and girl getting out of the Camaro. Shit. What were they doing here? My stomach knotted. I recognized the twins from a meeting I had followed my father to last week.

After he had met Avery, my father had been acting kind of strange. One night, while I was doing some homework in my room, he knocked on the door and said he was going to run an errand and would be gone an hour. I was concerned because he hadn't been acting like himself and would occasionally disappear at night.

That night I decided that I'd would see where he was going so I followed him to an office building just off of Main Street and across the train tracks. *This is not a good neighborhood*, I thought glancing around at the trash on the street. The building he stopped in front of was old with a couple of broken windows on the second floor. When my father got out of his car and approached the door, someone I didn't recognize let him in the building. Feeling apprehensive, I approached the building, but kept to the shadows. Headlights glanced off the window in front of me and I ducked down an alley, running quietly. There were windows down this wall, about a foot above me, but I stopped and gripped a windowsill straining to pull myself up to look inside.

The lights were dim, but I could see a group of men gathered around a set of chairs. My father was sitting in one, talking to a man about his age with blonde hair. They were sitting facing each other with their elbows on their knees, arguing quietly.

The door opened behind them and these two kids, both around my age, walked through. The girl was laughing and teasing the boy next to her. They both had the same coloring as the man my father was talking to and the boy looked like a younger version of him. Father and son, obviously.

My arms started to tremble, my fingers losing their grip on the windowsill and I dropped to the ground. Shaking my arms out I glanced around the alley and spotted a trash bin to one side. I picked it up, turned it over, and placed it beneath the window, then stepped onto it in a crouch, hoping they couldn't see me from the inside. This window had a piece of glass missing, so I could hear murmurs of conversation but no words specifically until my father raised his voice.

"No! That just can't be true, Julian!" My father shot up out of the chair and placed himself behind it, gripping the back of the chair.

Julian also stood from his chair and walked over to my father, placing a hand on his shoulder. "Mathis doesn't want to admit that it's true, because she's his daughter. But Will, you have admitted already that her powers have started building and she's not yet had her sixteenth birthday."

My father sank back into the chair shaking his head. "But my son, how am I going to tell him?" *Tell me what?* I thought, anxiously, wondering what my father was keeping from me.

"I know, we are all making sacrifices." Julian looked over to where his son and daughter stood inside the doorway watching them. "My son, Devon, too will be ready."

I glanced over their heads and made eye contact with Devon who had looked up and was staring directly at me. My adrenaline pumped as Devon turned back towards the door and I dropped down to the street and ran to my car. I started it and backed slowly away from the building, my headlights off, cruising down the street in the dark. Thankfully the streetlights weren't working or had been broken, because I noticed Devon coming out the front and looking around. I let out a breath, my heart a jackhammer in my chest and I gave a last glance back in my rearview mirror and turned the car around a corner and drove away.

When Devon and his sister got out of their Camaro in the parking lot at school, we made eye contact again. We held it for a few seconds, my hands clenching at my sides. The wind whipped a piece of hair onto my forehead and I reached up and swept it back, touching the bar in my eyebrow as I did. Electricity sizzled up my fingers, but I brought my hand back down and turned away pull open the door to go into school. *Keep your cool*, I thought. *You need to figure out what's going on, and fast.*

Chapter 11

Devon

I knew I was different when the other Elemental kids got their powers at twelve and I had already been able to mesmerize them by the time I was ten. You see, my father was a strong Elemental, having skills in both fire and air. However, his ambitions had always been larger than what those two powers offered.

His father had been Sentinel over the Committee in his day, with strength over three elements. As Sentinel, he had been allowed to marry outside of our race, choosing a human woman that he'd fallen in love with while at an Elemental gathering in Europe. That woman, however, was not an ordinary woman. The story was that my great-grandmother met my great-grandfather when she was part of a magical Vaudeville act in London.

As Sentinel, you are sent to visit other clans during annual Elemental gatherings. Each clan would strengthen ties with others around the world, helping out each other during troubled times. The London clan, as host of this Elemental gathering, hired a Vaudeville troupe to entertain one evening. There were various singers, dancers, and acrobats, and my great-grandmother had an act where she'd bring someone on stage and mesmerize them. Kind of like a hypnotist would do in shows today, except that my great-grandmother was a Mesmer. Once she mesmerized you, she stole a part of your will, so that she could call upon you to do her bidding whenever she wanted. At this party, she did not mesmerize anyone, because to mesmerize an Elemental was asking for more trouble than she'd want to bring upon herself. My great-grandmother's act on this night involved large cats that seemed tame and did tricks, but they were only tame for my great-grandmother. She had mesmerized each of them, and their will belonged to her.

The story I was told was that my grandfather and grandmother fell in love at first sight, and my grandfather used his influence in the clan to convince them to let him marry her. My grandmother's powers were inherited, but my father did not receive his mother's Mesmer powers, only his father's use of Fire and Air. Having two powers was a big deal, but he wasn't satisfied with having just two. His father and mother loved him unconditionally, and he grew to be a member of the Committee for our clan, but I think he was always resentful that he couldn't rise any higher.

When Dani and I were born, I started showing signs of the Mesmer skills at nine years old. My father was ecstatic. When I was twelve, I inherited my Elemental skills, receiving three of the powers, Air and Fire, like my father, and also Water. Having both Fire and Water was an extremely rare gift, because the two powers could cancel each other out if used incorrectly. He immediately enrolled me in training that would teach me how to use these gifts separately as well as together. No other boy in our clan received these two powers, and there was no one able to train me in both. My teachers had to group together, use their powers as a unit, and then figure out a way that Fire and Water could work for and against each other, and then teach me.

My sister, Dani, inherited Earth. It was rare for daughters to inherit any Elemental powers, and this gave my father another reason to boast. His daughter, not just his son, had inherited powers. Together, the two of us had all four powers, and we learned to use them both as weapons and in our own defense. In addition to her use of Earth, Dani proved to be an incredible athlete. She was able to run faster and farther than any other, climb and jump higher, and leap and tumble longer. It was almost as if she had inherited cat-like traits from my great-grandmother's pets. My mother enrolled her in gymnastics and track thinking that would be a good way to focus those talents, and she became the best athlete in our clan, including among the boys.

My grandmother, in her seventies, was the only Mesmer in the area. So She trained me to mesmerize without intent to capture anyone's will. Not wanting our entire clan to become mesmerized by me, she taught me to hypnotize and gain control, but then release my captives, with their will intact. I practiced this on animals until I became so good that at eleven, my father wanted me to try it on our cook. After successfully hypnotizing her without any harm, other than having her bake a houseful of my favorite treats, my grandmother deemed me a natural. Even though I had what she considered natural talent, she taught me that with this power came an awesome responsibility. It was not a power to use as a game. When she was first tutoring me in how to mesmerize and I was practicing on animals, I mesmerized my sister's pet dog by accident, transferring its favor from her to me. Once it was under my spell, I wasn't able to change the dog's favor back again, and my sister didn't forgive me for a long time.

She only forgave me when my mother made a promise to get her another puppy that I would never try to mesmerize.

My father, gifted with a talented son and daughter, began to push us harder in training and school, riding us to be the best. Dani took to that pressure better than I, easily surpassing anyone else in her class with her athletic skills as well as her element. However, it wasn't as important to me to be better than anyone else. I was fantastic at the elemental defense maneuvers but struggled a little bit more with the offensive skills. My father and I would often argue, and Dani would step between us if things became tense, diverting attention from me to her, successfully relieving the tension between the two of us. Because of this, my father favored Dani, but he pushed me harder. It was through me, he said, that he was going to rise through the ranks to Sentinel. I hated the pressure he put on me.

"Come in." I yelled, at the knock on my bedroom door. My sister opened it, with her phone to her ear.

"Okay, we'll be there in a half hour." She hung up and came over to stand next to me at my desk. "That was Dad. He wants us to meet him in town in a half hour." I made a face at her and she said, "Come on, it won't be that big a deal. He's meeting with a Committee member and wants us to be a part of their meeting." She flipped her long blonde hair over her shoulder and turned for the door.

"Wait. Did he give you any more information? I'm tired of being at his beck and call." I closed the book in front of me and pushed it aside with a shove. "Haven't you noticed how irrational he's been lately?"

"Irrational? Nah, he's always been intense, Devon. You know that! It's just how he is." She stepped over and sat down on the edge of the bed, balanced forward as if she was going to shoot up off it at any moment.

"Haven't you noticed how he's disappeared a lot lately, going to these secret meetings?" My fingers curled into imaginary quotation marks as I said "meetings" sarcastically. "I've asked Mom about it and I don't think she knows where he is either."

"Yeah, like she ever cares where he is." Dani rolled her eyes. Dani and our mom weren't seeing eye to eye lately. Dani had a lot of freedom because she was Dad's favorite, and no one could rein her in. Not even me. My father drove a wedge between us a long time ago, and whereas I loved her, I felt sad because I didn't really know her anymore.

"Why does it matter where he's been going if he's going to bring us in on the secret now?" She jumped up and strode to the door, throwing a "Hurry up!" over her shoulder.

I slowly stood up from my desk and grabbed my phone, shoved it into the back pocket of my jeans, and grabbed a sweatshirt. *Maybe she was right*, I thought. *If we're finally going to discover what the secret's all about, it might be worth being around the old man.*

I flicked my hand out and sent out a bolt to shut off my bedroom lights.

As we pulled up to the building, I looked at Dani. "This doesn't have you concerned?" I waved my hand around pointing. Even for our screwed up father, this was kind of a crazy. I had parked on a dark street across from an old brick warehouse. There was trash lining the streets, and a few of the buildings windows had been broken out. "Are you sure this is the right address?" I glanced down at my GPS to double check. Yep, I typed it in correctly glancing at the rundown building, one of many lining this street.

"Yes. Let's just go inside!" Dani snarled at me as she opened the door of her car.

In her eyes I was the bad guy, always questioning what our father asked us to do. I mean, I wanted to know how to use my powers, both Elemental and Mesmer, but I didn't want to blindly follow what anyone, even my own father, asked me to do. I wanted to know why. Was that unreasonable? According to Dani, it was. She didn't have a problem following our father's orders, but then he always came through for her. It was only me who received his empty promises. Mentally, I shrugged and followed my sister through the dilapidated door.

I wanted to get us back on the right foot so I grabbed my sister's arm and made a joke about the sunglasses on the guy who let us in, making her giggle in relief.

As we entered the room, I looked around. My father was seated on an ugly broken plaid couch talking to another man, who was seated in a chair facing him. He looked pretty shaken up. I didn't recognize him, so I looked at the other guys standing around, hoping their identities would clue me in. Nope. I didn't know any of these guys, and I wondered how I missed the memo on the dress code. They were all in white button-downs and dark slacks with sunglasses. I looked back over to the couch when the man my dad was talking to stood up abruptly, exclaiming loudly. Normally I would have totally found this interesting but something outside the window on the other side of the room caught my eye.

Is that? Yes, there was a kid around my age, with black hair and a piercing through his eyebrow staring through the window, obviously eavesdropping. We made eye contact and his head disappeared. What the hell? I raced back through the door behind me, just in time to see an old car take off down the street. Huh. *Well, that was really strange*, I thought.

I went back inside to see Dani watching the argument between our dad and this other man. "Have you figured out what they're talking about?" I whispered to her.

"Nope. They have mentioned the Sentinel's name though." Of course, Dani being Dani, she looked excited about the drama.

At that moment, my father looked up and saw us standing by the door. "Devon, Dani, would you please come over here? There's someone I'd like you to meet." He put a hand on the other man's arm and spoke quietly to him. I heard my name mentioned.

"Devon, Dani, this is Will Sullivan." When I reached out my hand to Mr. Sullivan, I noticed the air start to stir dust across the floor. Surprised, I put out a hand and soothed the wind back down. *Something must've really upset this guy for him to get out of control like that*, I thought.

"Devon. Dani. Nice to meet you." He shook both our hands and then collapsed back onto the chair where he had been sitting. The air swirled again, pushing past him and out the broken glass window, leaving behind a slight chill. My father gestured to two folding chairs close by asking us to take a seat. I noticed the other men in the room had moved in front of the windows and doors to the room, blocking all of the entrances–or was it our exit?

I didn't take a seat, instead turning instead back towards my father, trying to gauge his mood. "What's going on Dad?" Dani was sitting in one of the chairs twisting her hair around her index finger while looking curiously around the room, waiting to do our fathers bidding like a dutiful daughter, I suppressed a sigh.

"Will has news about the Sentinel's daughter being found in Dover." My father's serious tone had Dani and I exchanging glances.

"His daughter? You mean." I stopped myself from saying the rest of the sentence. Since Mathis had come back and was now Sentinel of the Committee no one talked openly about the prophecy. At least not to us kids.

"Yes, apparently his wife has died and his daughter Avery has shown up in Dover, where her aunt is living." As my father spoke, I looked at Mr. Sullivan. He had his elbows on his knees and his hands were combing through his hair. He was wrecked.

"She showed up a month ago, but my son, Cole, only told me about her last week." He exchanged a look with my father and continued, "It's true what they are saying; I've seen it for myself. Her powers have already started manifesting and she's not even sixteen yet!" At that news, Dani sat up on the couch, looking excited and even I jerked in interest.

"Devon, Dani, we are going to enroll you in Dover High. We want you to keep an eye on things and gather more information." My father put his hand on Dani's shoulder and looked me in the eye. "If her powers are manifesting, we may need you close so you can contain her." Dani looked way too excited about this information. I however, had my doubts.

"Contain her? You mean restrict her powers somehow?" I asked carefully.

"We'll see, but there's a strong possibility that the situation may be even more dire." I could see my father squeezing Dani's shoulder to keep her in her seat.

"Awesome, finally, a mission that will give us the chance to show what we can do, Devon!" Dani had moved out from under my father's grasp and moved towards me, stopping in front of me. Energy was coming off of her in waves and I could see the water in the glasses start to sway gently.

"Get control of yourself," I whispered harshly to her. I turned back towards my father, trying to make eye contact with him, but he pulled out a pair of sunglasses and put them on before facing me.

"Come on, Dad! You really think I'm going to try to mesmerize you? I just want some answers! This whole thing seems kind of drastic. What do you mean by containing her? Are you talking about killing her? Are you nuts?" Yes, my father and I didn't see eye to eye, but this seemed really out of character! And what was he thinking with the glasses? I would never abuse my Mesmer powers. I felt hurt that he'd think I'd use those powers against him.

As an Elemental, I was trained in both defense and offense, but Elementals were meant to protect, not destroy. Many of us became Guardians, which was what I was hoping to do after I got out of school, not kill young girls! With a sinking pit in my stomach, I realized my father was serious.

Mr. Sullivan answered before my father could. "It's just a precaution, Devon. Cole is already in place as her Guardian, but I think he's becoming emotionally involved. If we need to make a tough decision, I'm not sure he'll be able to keep his emotions out of it."

"Well, that won't be a problem for us, will it, Devon." Dani stated as she bounced on her toes excitedly.

I frowned at her. "No. No problem," I answered sarcastically, looking at my father as he nodded in approval.

"Glad to hear it, son."

Chapter 12

Avery

I was sitting next to Summer in first period English, twisted around in my seat, so I could talk to both Ana and her at the same time. We were going over our notes because Mr. Newsome had just announced we were having a pop quiz. I stole a glance behind Ana to where Cole was sitting. He had earbuds in and his fingers were tapping the top of the desk. He caught my eye and gave me a small smile. The door to the classroom opened behind me and I heard Ana give a small gasp. I noticed Cole reach up to pull the earbuds out of his ears as he straightened up in his seat, looking forward. I turned around in my seat to see why everyone had reacted so strongly.

Standing in front of Mr. Newsome's desk was a very good-looking guy. He was tall, about 5′10″, with blonde hair, wearing jeans and a blue t-shirt. I felt a warm current run through the air and he turned his head and looked over his shoulder directly into my eyes. His were glowing a bright blue. As Mr. Newsome cleared his throat, the boy slowly turned his head until he was facing the class, his eyes still holding mine.

"Class, it looks like we have a new student. Devon, why don't you introduce yourself?" Devon glanced around at the class, his gaze stopping on someone behind me briefly, and then coming back to rest on me. Our eyes caught and held, as he addressed the room and my breath caught in my throat.

"My name is Devon Finn. My family just moved here from Northern California and I have a twin sister Dani, who's also starting school here today." His voice was low and husky and the class seemed to be motionless. I know I was. As he motioned to an empty desk in the back of the room, I fought to close my eyes. Why was I having trouble focusing? I blinked and opened them to see Mr. Newsome nodding to his unasked question.

He started moving down the aisle toward the open seat in the back of the class. As he passed by me, the pencil I had been holding jerked out of my hand and hit the floor in front of him. I looked down in astonishment as he paused and knelt down on the ground to pick it up, maintaining eye contact with me the entire time. I felt a blush work its way up my throat when I heard a throat clearing behind me, and I knew it was Cole trying to gain Devon's attention. Devon glanced over at Cole and stood up, holding the pencil out towards me with his left hand and a small smile on his face.

My eyes were caught by the glint of light off a silver ring he wore. It had initials engraved on the top, and I twisted my head to try to read them. Without thinking I reached out a finger to touch it and felt my own ring start to tingle. I pulled my hand back and grabbed my pencil, a breeze lifted my hair across my lips. I felt the ground rumble slightly as I carefully put the pencil back on my desk, and I tucked my hair behind my ears to get it to stay still, my fingers shaking. His lips tilted up slightly and he continued to walk to the back of the room. My eyes followed him until he sat down, giving me a smile when he saw that I was still looking at him.

Guiltily, my eyes flew to Cole, who was watching Devon walk away. Cole wore a slight frown on his face and his hands gripped the book in front of him tightly. I exchanged looks with Ana who looked mildly interested in what just happened. She raised her eyebrows at me and I noticed the freckles on her skin were swirling, as if trying to decide if there was a threat in the room. I looked over at Summer, who shrugged and gave me a "what was that?" look. Uncomfortable, I shrugged back and reached forward automatically to take the quiz that was being passed back to me.

After class was over I started to get out of my seat and grabbed my backpack off the floor to put my books inside. I looked for Devon in the back of the room and noticed he was gone already. I shrugged off my disappointment and looked at Cole as he and Ben walked up to Summer, Ana, and I.

"There's something funny about that guy showing up right now." Cole said to Ben. I noticed his eyes scanning the room and wondered what he was looking for.

"Did you notice that ring he was wearing?" I asked them, remembering the initials, "It's almost exactly like the one I wear, but silver, instead of gold." I didn't know if our rings looking similar had any significance, but I agreed with Cole. With my birthday coming up, I wasn't leaving anything to chance, Devon showing up right before my birthday seemed like more than accidental timing.

"My ring tingled slightly when he handed me my pencil and that wasn't the only strange thing. I didn't drop my pencil, it was like it was yanked out of my hand." I exchanged a look with Summer, "And that eye contact!" I shivered remembering his piercing blue eyes.

"Sugar, maybe he just thought you were cute!" Summer teased.

I shrugged. I didn't think that was it. There was chemistry, but what I felt was something different. I am definitely putting him into the questionable category, even with his all-American good looks.

Cole looked at the clock, "We need to get to second period, but I'll see you at lunch." He looked at Ana, "Both of you keep an eye out for his twin sister. He mentioned her name was Dani?" I nodded as Summer, Ben, and Cole moved off down the hall to their classes. Ana and I walked towards Biology and I asked her about our biology homework, knowing the excitement of that class would distract her. Sure enough, Ana bubbled with enthusiasm as she told me her thoughts.

As we entered our Biology class, my attention was immediately caught by a small crowd of girls gathered together around one of the lab stations. A couple of the girls were on the cheerleading squad, and today being Friday, were wearing their cheerleading uniforms. They were excitedly talking to a new girl who was standing at the center of their group. She was small, probably 5′1″," but had long blonde hair and a pair of familiar electric blue eyes. She looked up at Ana and me as we entered the room but continued talking animatedly with the other girls. We sat down at our lab station, overhearing the conversation at the table next to us. *That must be Dani*, I thought and pointed her out to Ana, who agreed.

"She said she was a cheerleader at the school she's transferring from, and she's a gymnast!" one of the cheerleaders gushed to the other.

I looked at Ana. "Didn't one of the cheerleaders have some kind of nervous breakdown and quit a couple days ago?" Not that I paid a lot of attention to that group since they were kind of cliquish and very popular. However, a nervous breakdown isn't that normal, and everyone had been talking about it.

The two girls continued to talk excitedly about tryouts and the game next Friday.

"It does seem kind of coincidental," Ana said quietly, looking worried when I agreed. Her freckles were whirling madly across her skin, making her skin tone change color between the grey of the table and chairs around us, to the beige of the walls.

Our teacher, Ms. Hollander, introduced the new student as Dani and once again we heard the same short speech her brother gave in first period. As Dani spoke she excitedly twirled her hair around her finger and tapped a foot on the ground. At a word from our teacher she started moving towards our table. Her bright blue eyes focused on me with interest. I could feel Ana fidget next to me and quickly glanced over at her. She had turned the grey of our table. Figuring one of us needed to be strong, I pat her hand and gave it a squeeze.

"Hi!" Dani whispered. She reached out a hand, which I noticed also wore a silver ring with initials on it. I'm not sure why, but I ignored Ana's whispered "Don't," and reached my own hand out to shake hers. Our rings touched together as we clasped hands and the tingle I normally felt changed immediately to a jolt and an electric shock raced between us, our eyes locking together. I gasped in shock but noticed Dani only smiled happily.

Like my English class, our Biology class was in a room with windows along one side overlooking the open quad area. Even though all of the windows were closed, I felt a breeze race through the classroom, whipping papers loose from their binders to create a whirlwind. The other kids scrambled to grab onto their paperwork but gave up quickly and ran out of the classroom, yelling. Dani and I still held hands, but it had turned from a friendly hello, to something more intense. Both of our grips were strong, neither one of us loosening our grasp. My eyes narrowed on hers, not liking that crazy look in her eyes.

Against the flow of students leaving through the door in the back of the classroom, I noticed Cole out of the corner of my eye, shoving his way into the class. “Let go!” He yelled, as he ran towards us. The ground shook slightly and he stumbled.

I heard him yell, but I felt something happening inside of me that I couldn’t ignore. Energy was building up that needed some kind of release. I looked into Dani’s eyes, and saw that she no longer looked as happy and engaging as she did when we first caught sight of her, she looked at me with caution, which was rapidly turning into anger. I felt that power burn to be let go however I wasn’t sure how to do that and not hurt her. At this point, I was pretty sure I didn’t want to be her friend, but I also didn’t want to make an enemy.

I flicked my left hand out at her, while still holding her with my right. I felt a barrier go up between us ripping my hand from her grasp. Cole tugged me backwards and I fell into his chest. He wrapped an arm around me and pushed me slightly behind him, but I didn’t want his protection and moved to his side.

Through the door at the front of the classroom, I saw Devon. He had stopped just inside the room taking in everything at a glance. He focused on Dani and started moving towards her, as he did, I saw him pull something out of the pocket of his jeans and touch it to the invisible wall. I felt a small pop reverberate through my head and he reached out for his sister, asking a question, softly.

We were at a stand-off. The two of them faced Cole and I. A flurry of movement behind me made me tear my eyes away from Devon and look over my shoulder to see Summer and Ben. Ana stepped forward from the wall she had been blending into to join them behind us. I slowly breathed out unclenching my hands and shaking out my fingers.

"Well, this is interesting," Dani said to Devon. "I don't believe sharing a table with her is going to work." As Dani said "her," she looked over at me. Her eyes were a freaky light ice blue color, with only a small pinprick of black for the pupils. Even though the wind had died down in the classroom her hair, and Devon's, shifted with a breeze only they could feel. My hair remained still, but the ground rumbled a warning.

Cole grabbed my hand and I jerked my eyes away from Devon who smiled broadly as if we'd shared a joke. I wasn't sure what I was feeling, but I knew I didn't feel like laughing. I turned to my friends and said, "Come on, let's get out of here."

Ms. Hollander chose that moment to step back into the classroom with the Principal. "There must've been a window open or something," she said in explanation. The classroom was a wreck, with chairs overturned and papers littering the floor. Looking flustered, Ms. Hollander looked at us and said, "Please go into the auditorium with the rest of the school."

We all looked at each other and nodded in agreement. I made an after you gesture to Devon and he bowed slightly back at me, still smiling. We waited for them to walk out of the classroom and we followed slowly behind. I whispered with Ana and Summer about what had happened with our rings, a little proud that I had not let Dani dominate me with her power.

At lunch that day, I watched Devon and Dani sit beneath a tree, while kids from various groups introduced themselves. *Is this normal?* I thought as the cheerleading squad energetically tried to recruit Dani to try out that afternoon for the open position on their team. My eyes were glued to Devon who reclined back against the trunk of the tree, talking to a group of boys on the surf team. Every once in awhile our eyes would lock and he'd grin and hold my gaze until I looked away. *What was with that guy?* I thought to myself as I slowly ate my sandwich.

"That guy gives me the creeps," Ana said quietly. I nodded slowly because he did make me feel slightly uneasy, but creepy? I didn't really think he was creepy but I wasn't sure how I felt yet. We had just finished re-telling Cole and Ben about what had happened in Biology. I looked over at Cole.

"You've been training as a Guardian for four years, right?" I asked.

"Yeah." He answered cautiously.

"Is there anything you can teach me to counteract that hold she had on me?" I was proud that I had managed to break her hold with a shield but wanted a little bit more control.

Summer sat forward, looking towards Cole. "There must be something additional you can teach her," she said. Ben laid his hand on her back and nodded at Cole.

"Dude, tell her what you told me last night," Ben said.

Cole nodded. "My Dad doesn't want to give you any higher level of training, but after today, I think I should start Guardian level training with you. We have already determined what kind of powers you have but after today, I think you need some more control exercises." He looked around at our group. "Are you all still cool, meeting at her Aunt's shop after school? I'm going to need your help."

Everyone nodded, except for Ana who had to decorate the gym for the dance, which was next Friday. We all agreed to meet at four o'clock and Cole and I walked together to our next class. I was amped from what happened earlier and eager to learn something new. When I mentioned that to Cole, he nodded quietly, and repeated that he was going to be teaching me against his father's wishes. I could tell Cole didn't like going against the rules so I bumped his shoulder and grinned, trying to tease him out of the funk he was in. Funny, even though Cole had that eyebrow piercing and looked to be a rebel, he really was a good son, following his father's orders. I remembered my confusion at my own mothers actions half the time and even though I'd do what she wanted, none of it every really made since. I felt myself tense up at the memory. I really missed her even though our relationship was pretty messed up. I was really enjoying being more settled and having a normal life. Well, as normal as I could be in a high school with a bunch of Other kids.

Chapter 13

Devon

Rumor had it that every year Newsome made the Sophomore class pair up and recite scenes from Romeo and Juliet for an assignment. After spending the past few days having Avery avoid me, I needed a good excuse to get to know her a little bit better. Dani was convinced she was a power-hungry bitch, but I was starting to think otherwise. On the surface, she seemed like any normal girl. I mean, you take away the power that she has exhibited, and she seems kind of shy and sweet.

I walked up to the front of the room to hand in my homework before class started, and thought I'd give Newsome a push into pairing up Avery and me.

"Devon, you have exhibited a real grasp of Shakespeare's language." Newsome said as he looked up from my paperwork, marking the top with an A+.

"Thanks, sir," I said. I let my hand rise up slowly to take the papers from him, and waved it slightly, so the lights glinted off the silver initials in my ring. I used stored power I gathered from the sun this morning surfing and sent a push towards him. "You are going to assign the teams for the Romeo and Juliet assignment today." I made it a statement, sub vocally inserting my demand that Avery be my partner and held Newsome's gaze until I felt a small click.

"I am going to make the assignment, yes." Newsome looked through me and shook his head. "What was I saying?"

"It sounded like you said something about an assignment?" I said as I turned grinning and started for my seat. I heard Mr. Newsome's voice rise behind me.

"Class. As we have finished reading Romeo and Juliet, I have a new assignment to announce." He announced and the students groaned. He waved a hand in dismissal. "Yes, Yes. Settle down." He looked down at a piece of paper in front of him and narrowed his eyes in confusion. I watched him scratch off two lines and re-write them.

"The assignment is for you and a partner to pick a scene from Romeo and Juliet and recite it in front of the class. We have permission to use the auditorium on the day of the recitations, so I expect a bit of dramatic skill with your efforts." When he finished, there were groans from the guys around the room, but some of the girls whispered to each other in excitement.

I glanced over at Avery and her friends and saw they were whispering as well. One of her friends looked anxious, and I noticed her skin changed to match the color of the walls. *Well now, that's interesting*, I thought.

"Here are the pairings," and Newsome started reading off some names. There were squeals and moans when names were mentioned. I waited until I heard mine, then smiled in satisfaction.

"Devon will read with Avery," Mr. Newsome said. I was looking at Avery when her name was read and saw her gasp. Summer reached over and touched her arm. I glanced at Cole and saw that his teeth grit with anger. Newsome continued, "Cole will read with Ana," I saw

Cole's fist clench and then relax. Ana, the girl whose skin changed color, looked over at him and nodded. He turned in his seat and glared at me.

"You have a week to memorize and practice, so spend the next twenty-five minutes with your partner to pick your verses." Newsome said and sat back down in his chair, gazing blankly at the paper in front of him.

I cleared my throat and spoke Avery's name. I saw her jump slightly, but then turn towards me. "Do you want to come over here? Or me there?" I asked. She glanced at her friends, then reached to pick up her backpack to move over to the desk next to me.

"Uh, hi." She said glancing over her shoulder at her friends again.

I said hi back, then thought I'd just act normal. I opened up my book and started searching for a section to read. "Do you have any ideas about what part of the book you want to read from?" I asked and looked up and caught her staring at me in bewilderment. "Avery? The assignment?"

"Oh, yeah, the assignment." She opened up her own book and bent her head towards me slightly. She smelled of lemons and green grass, and I took in a breath.

I opened my book and skimmed through to the part where Romeo finds Juliet on the balcony. I read through it and look at her. "I like the section where Juliet does the Romeo, Romeo wherefore art thou, but a little past that part where they speak of her being a Capulet, and him a Montague. I kind of understand how he feels." I said this last part under my breath.

I heard a small gasp and I look up to find her giving me a confused look. "What do you mean?" She asked.

I shrug embarrassed that she heard that comment and pretended like I didn't hear her. I asked when she'd like to get together to start memorizing this piece.

"Um, I can do it after practice. Do you want to meet in the library?" she asks uncertainly, and I see her glance over towards her friends. I see Cole staring hard in our direction, pretty much ignoring Ana sitting quietly next to him.

"Perfect." I quickly gather my things and get up from the desk just as the bell rings for next period. "I'll see you later." I walk out the door, as if life is normal, and this cute girl I've just set a study date with isn't a possible threat to my world.

I glance impatiently at my watch again. It's past 4:30, she should've finished with soccer practice a half hour ago. In frustration, I start to gather my stuff together to shove into my backpack. I hear the library door whoosh open and look up. Avery is rushing through the doors, looking worried. I sit back down and put my notes back on the table.

"Sorry!" she whispered to me as she slid into the seat across from me. "Practice was, well, I'm sorry I'm late."

"Cole giving you a hard time?" I grinned at her boldly.

"What? No. I mean, it doesn't matter, really." She glanced over her shoulder when the door opened and Summer and Ana strolled in. They sat down at the next table.

"Reinforcements? Really?" I gave her an innocent look and shrug, cracking the book open.

She looked slightly embarrassed, and then smiled. "You've just been, well, a little intimidating, that's all."

I stopped smiling. Intimidating? I hadn't meant to be intimidating. I was just trying to figure her out, but of course I couldn't tell her that. "If it makes you feel better, then I'm all for this," I said waving my hand at her friends. I saw her look down at my ring, then reach her hand across to her own.

"Do you mind if I ask you a question?" she asked.

I shook my head, in what I hoped was an encouraging manner. "Sure, what about?"

"Well, you and I seem to have the same ring, though mine's gold and yours is well, silver." She put her hand on the table and I placed my hand next to hers. My ring started to become warm on my hand and I looked curiously at it.

"Can you feel that?" I whispered to her in shock. I've never felt this ring gather heat like it was right now.

"Yeah. When Dani and I shook hands that first time, our rings had a reaction to each other. What do you think it means?" As she looked at me I marveled over how her hazel eyes were turning green in wonder.

"If you want, I can look it up in our library at home. My father gave me this ring when I inherited my powers when I turned twelve. This, and the one Dani wears, has been in the family for ages, so we're bound to have more information on it." I reached over and touched my hand to hers. The heat turned into a warm electric hum. Not a jolt like it had given Dani. I slowly withdrew my hand and looked over to her friends who were watching us.

Avery looked at them also and shook her head slightly. "Okay, maybe we should start our assignment," she said.

I nodded in agreement, deciding that there was more to this girl than I was being told and maybe more to why Dani and I were picked to watch her?

We all left the library together, Avery walking between her friends and me. It seemed as though peace had been made between us, for the moment, and I was enjoying it.

As we crossed the empty quad towards the exit to the parking lot, something made me look over my shoulder up at the roofline. I stopped, and Avery and her friends stopped with me.

"What the hell?" I turned around quickly and pushed Avery behind me. I heard her grumble something like "I wish they'd stop doing that!" but focused on the rooftop next to us.

Across the top of the building were six men in white button down shirts, black slacks, and sunglasses. Shocked, I realized they were dressed exactly like the men who had been at the meeting with my father. Avery pushed against my back and stepped around me.

"They look just like the man who came into my aunt's shop!" she said to Summer and Ana. She shrugged out of her backpack and placed it on the ground. Summer and Ana followed suit.

"I think I've seen them somewhere before too." I mentioned quietly setting my own books on the ground to start gathering energy to me in preparation.

"Ana, get back against that wall and disappear!" Avery hissed, pushing Ana behind her. Ana didn't argue and melted against the wall until I couldn't see her anymore. *Cool trick*, I thought, before glancing back at the men.

"Get on the phone for help!" Avery continued to direct her friend, and I could hear soft mumbling from behind me.

"On it," Ana whispered.

"Sugar, I don't mean to shock you, but I'm going to get ready for trouble." Summer pushed her backpack behind her, shrugged out of her jacket, and kicked off her shoes.

I looked at her in shock as hair started to sprout out of her arms, her face started shifting, and her hands and feet developed claws. After fully shifting, she had grown in height by about three inches. She shook out her hair, opened her mouth and hissed, showing off all of her fangs.

I heard a thud in front of me and looked back up to see the men jumping off the second-floor roof to the ground in front of us. I shook my hands out, feeling Avery move up beside me. I reached out my hand to push her back again, but when our rings touched, a loud crack shocked through the air, and the wind started whipping about.

"Okay, you're good where you are." I dropped her hand and let her step up.

"Six to three. Not bad odds," Summer spoke up, and hissed again. "I had worse odds at my last family reunion."

I heard a little giggle from behind us. "Cole's on the way," Ana whispered.

"I think he might miss the party," I said.

"Who are these guys?" Avery's hair started to whip in the wind she was creating. Her hand was moving in a slow circle, and the sun started to intensify its rays into the path of one of the men. She flung out a hand and the glasses fell off the man's head, showing eyes that burned like red fire.

I took in a shocked breath. "Daïmonids!" I spoke harshly and took a step forward.

"Devon, you can explain that later." Summer sank to her haunches, and sprang at one of the Daïmonids, slashing out with her claws. I heard his scream as I rushed forward to help.

"Don't look them in the eyes, they can blind you!" I yelled. I punched a fist forward and hit a Daïmonid in the face and then swung my hand out towards the water fountain on the wall behind him. With some effort, I pulled water through those pipes with enough force that the top of the fountain exploded, shooting metal shrapnel towards me. I ducked, and heard a man scream. Looking up, I saw a piece of metal sticking out of the top of one of their heads before he exploded in a pop and disappeared. I heard Avery scream next to me and saw her swing her arm up and create a shield, while at the same time ripping up a clod of dirt behind the Daïmonid she was facing and rack him in the back of the head with it, bringing him to his knees. *Nice move*, I thought.

With my energy, I pushed the water stream towards the Daïmonid, and as it hit him he screamed in agony and fizzled away. Out of the corner of my eye, I saw movement and was about to swing my arm up when Summer leaped through the air and pushed the Daïmonid to the side. He landed awkwardly but managed to send a laser beam towards Avery that she shielded against.

"Avery!" I yelled at her and swung my hand over towards her as far as I could reach. "Take my hand! I think together, the power in our rings could take them out!" Without hesitation she reached out her hand and grasped mine, and a powerful boom shook the earth. The light bulbs in all the hallways burst, and a lightning bolt hit the earth, melting the remaining Daïmonids into dust.

In the silence that followed, I could hear a car door slam, and running footsteps. Cole ran into the quad to find all of us panting in relief, and Avery and I holding hands. Instinctively I tightened my hold and felt a responding squeeze hard enough to make me look away from Cole. He glanced from our joined hands to Avery's flushed face. Then mine. Out of the corner of my eye, I saw movement, and noticed my sister on the rooftop, taking a step back so that she couldn't be seen. What the hell? I was definitely going to find out why my sister was watching her brother fight Daïmonid ass! I looked back at Cole hoping he hadn't noticed.

"Well, that was fun," I said sarcastically. "Care to fill us in on what's going on?" I gave Avery's hand another quick squeeze and then let go. My sister was going to have to wait.

The girls cancelled their shopping trip and we all went to Gino's to talk and grab a bite to eat. Summer looked like she could gnaw someone's arm off, literally. Ben was at Gino's when we got there and Summer slid into the booth next to him. He murmured in her ear and she responded, "I'm all right, Sugar. But I'd really like to know who those fellas were." Ana, seated at her side, nodded in agreement, the freckles on her face whirling madly.

Somehow, I ended up in the booth against the wall next to Avery with Cole on the other side of her. *Cozy*, I thought and slung my arm across the back of the booth behind Avery shifting forward so I could see Cole. He looked at my arm, raised an eyebrow at me, and spoke to the group. With Ben's help, they told the story of their own Daïmonid encounter after the soccer game, and what one of them had said.

After the girls gave them a hard time over keeping that secret, I asked Cole, "So, just to clarify, your theory is that the Daïmonid faction thinks Avery is going to banish Avdar? That they're trying to get rid of her before she can do that?"

"And I'm supposed to know how to do this, how?" Avery interjected lookling frustrated. I reached out to touch her hand, but at Cole's glare I took my time pulling it back into my lap, but not before I sent a little warmth her way. Avery looked warily at me, but didn't move away, which I thought was a positive sign.

"Aves, it seems like everything you've done so far has been instinctive. It could be that you don't even have to know how to send him back. Just that you are strong enough to be able to do it is threat enough," Summer said looking at Avery in concern, and then unsurprisingly reached for another slice of pizza.

"Well, waiting for my father to tell me is taking too long. And truthfully," Cole looked at Devon meaningfully, "he may have his own agenda. I think we need to develop our own plan. Devon, I appreciate the help today, but I'll take it from here." He reached up and shoved my arm off the back of the seat.

"Hey!" I reached up to hit the back of his head, but Avery elbowed me in the side.

I settled into my corner of the booth rubbing my side. "I'm not going anywhere until I know she's gotten home safe." I nodded at Avery and glared at Cole over her head.

Chapter 14

Cole

That night when I got home, I confronted my father with what had happened.

"Dad, the Sentinel needs to know that Avery's life is in danger! Surely he would want to see to her safety?" I looked at my father in frustration. He was sitting at the desk in his office drinking whiskey out of a highball. He slugged back another drink and looked at me through bloodshot eyes.

"He knows," he answered, reluctantly.

"What do you mean he knows? Isn't he worried?" I asked. I raked a hand through my hair, but only succeeded in making it fall over my forehead.

"Cole, Mathis called earlier and changed our mission," my father said slowly. He took another drink, and then set the glass on the table. He unsteadily got up from the chair and walked around his desk until he was standing in front of me.

"Son, with everything you've told us, he is worried that the prophecy is coming true. Avery is already too powerful, and she only has some of her Elemental powers. Once she starts to enter her transition–"

"If she even does!" I interrupted, yelling in his face. I couldn't believe what I was hearing.

"Mathis has made the most difficult decision of his life. She's his daughter, Cole. If she is the beginning of the end for the Elemental and Seer kind, then she needs to be destroyed." He looked into my eyes and seeing my confusion quickly looked down at the ground.

"What?" I whispered, shocked. I turned away from my father and stared blankly at the wall. "But, I'm her Guardian," I whispered. This went against everything that I've ever been trained. We serve to protect!

"You have been relieved of Guardian duty, Cole. Your new mission is to kill her before her sixteenth birthday. We can't afford to have her strong enough that the prophecy comes true." My body jerked at the word kill coming out of my father's mouth.

"But what about vanquishing Avdar?" *Surely if she's powerful enough to doom us, then she's definitely powerful enough to banish Avdar,* I thought. "We were counting on her help!"

"Yes, we were. We'll have to find another way to take care of Avdar, but the immediate threat is Avery."

Threat? This is crazy, I thought. "She's a sweet girl! She doesn't really even know how to use her powers and even if she did, she'd never knowingly harm anyone." I was practically pleading with my father. This couldn't be happening.

"And you will stop teaching her anything important." My father clapped me on the back. "I know this will not be an easy task, but I trust you to follow the correct path. For our family and all Elementals."

Looking at my father trying to smile at me with confidence I felt sick. Without a word, I turned away and walked out of the room. I threw the screen door open with a loud crash and walked off the back deck toward the woods lining our property. *What were they thinking?* I thought, picturing Avery's sweet smile.

The pine needles crunched under my feet as I approached the clearing. Years ago, someone had created a circle with stones piled around like groupings of furniture. I climbed onto one and sat down, my thoughts circling around in my head. *Kill her? I'm not sure I can do this*, I thought.

My father had been acting strange lately, but I couldn't see him going against the Sentinel's wishes. The pine trees surrounding the clearing swayed in the breeze and I flung an arm wide in frustration and heard a crack. A limb crashed to the ground a few feet away. I got up off the rock and paced the circle, watching the pine needles scatter away from my footsteps.

Was it possible that the Sentinel would destroy his own daughter to save our races? I shook my head. It seemed farfetched, but it was possible. My Guardian instincts flared, and I glanced over my shoulder. A blackbird, similar to the one I've seen with Avery's aunt landed on a branch in front of me. A golden haze enveloped the bird and a man in a dark business suit with a dark red tie stood where the bird had been.

Recognizing him immediately, I knelt on the ground, with my head bowed in respect, "Sir."

"There isn't a need for formality, Cole. Please get up." The Sentinel, Mathis waited for me to rise, clasped my shoulder and then indicated that we should continue our walk down the path.

"Your father has said that he's talked to you, and that you were having trouble with your new mission." He looked down at his feet and then back up at me. "I know you and Avery have gotten close?"

I nodded my head. "She's a friend, and, well, I like her too." We walked along in silence and then Mathis came to a stop. "I'm glad she has had a good friend. Her life has not been easy up to this point. Her mother and I had such huge dreams, and I'm afraid that they just weren't very realistic." His jaw clenched and he looked away.

I stared hard at him, trying to read what he was feeling. I mean, seriously? He was talking about destroying his daughter, and he seemed only slightly upset.

"Sir, are you bothered by the fact that you are asking me to kill your daughter?" In my frustration, the earth fell away from in front of us, creating a small hole. I breathed out, trying to gain some control as Mathis spun around to face me.

"Of course this bothers me! She's my daughter! But we have learned that there is another faction who will try to steal her powers from her after she inherits them during her transition on the night of her sixteenth birthday." As Mathis spoke, clouds flew across the sky, covering the sun, creating darkness where we stood. He blew out a breath and straightened the lapel on his coat.

"If this other faction steals her powers, then we will never have enough strength to deliver Avdar back to his dimension. If this faction steals her powers and delivers them to Avdar, then our lives, and those of all Others, will be over." The strength of his determination showed on his face, and the agony of his decision was in his eyes.

"I made a promise to her mother that I would protect Avery, and in this way I am. If her powers are stolen from her, she will live in a coma for the rest of her life, and all Elementals will be dead," he said grimly. "Do you now understand the importance of this mission? All Elementals are relying on you. Your father and I are both relying on you." Mathis looked straight into my eyes, looking for understanding, and through the churning in my mind and gut I gave it to him.

"Yes, sir. I understand." I spoke quietly, conviction settling in my voice. My heart beating heavily in my chest with dread.

"Thank you, Cole." He placed a hand on my shoulder and squeezed it gently. Just as he said those words the sun came back out. His body shimmered in a haze of heat, and a blackbird with red stripes on its wings flew away into the sky.

Chapter 15

Avery

The next day after our soccer game, Summer, Ana, and I were walking away from the field and I was surprised to see Cole's car driving out of the lot in the distance.

"Sugar, did you guys have a fight?" Summer looked at me in concern but looked over at Ben with a smile when he walked up to join us.

"No. I'm not sure what's going on. He hasn't talked to me all day." Truthfully, I'd been confused by how he's been acting. He had been absent from first period that morning, and didn't eat lunch with us, which was kind of weird. I looked over at Ben and raised my eyebrows.

Ben shrugged, "I don't have a clue." He gave Summer a kiss on the cheek, nodded at us, and ran off to his car.

"Strange." Ana, said quietly at my side. I looked at her and nodded in agreement. "I'll see what I can find out if you want?"

Not thinking too much of it, I responded halfheartedly, "Yeah, sure." Ana quietly excused herself with a "see you later" and walked quickly to her car.

"Are you still meeting up with Devon tonight?" Summer asked with a smile in her voice. After our battle with the Daïmonids and Devon fighting at our side, Summer seemed to have changed her mind from her first impression of him, though she still didn't like his sister much. Neither did I. Dani always seemed to be around watching us, and it was kind of creepy.

"Yeah, he should be around here somewhere." I looked over at the parking lot and saw him standing by his car. I gave him a quick wave, smiled and said goodbye to Summer.

Devon pushed away from the car as I walked up to him. "Hey," I said quietly, watching his face to gage his mood.

"Hi." His smiled started slow but built into a grin. "I saw your boyfriend blow out of here kind of quick. I thought he didn't let you go anywhere alone," he teased.

"Well, he's not my boyfriend, so obviously that isn't a problem." I snapped. Truthfully, it had kind of hurt that Cole hadn't talked to me at school all day.

"Hey, I'm just glad to have you all to myself." Devon opened the passenger door and swept his hand out in an "after you" gesture.

I peeked into his Camaro, which was surprisingly clean, and noticed some bags from a local deli in the back seat. I turned a questioning look his way.

"I picked up some food because I figured you might be hungry after practice." He nodded again towards the car, and I got in the passenger seat kind of pleased that he was making such an effort.

"Thanks," I said. I actually was kind of hungry and I wasn't really sure where things stood with Cole. I looked over at him as he got in the car, curious. "Where are we going?"

"I know a place down by the beach. The weather is great, so why not study outdoors?" He said as we pulled away from the school and got on the freeway heading towards the coast, only a twenty minute drive away.

As we hauled our stuff down to the sand I took a look out at the water. This was the first time I had been to the beach since moving in with my aunt. No car meant no way to get there, unfortunately.

As we put our stuff on the corners of the blanket Devon had brought from the car, I noticed him watching the surfers out in the water.

"Do you surf?" I asked, not really surprised when I thought about it. He certainly looked like he did, with the tan and blonde sun streaked hair. Then I remembered him hanging out with the surfers at school and winced. Dumb question.

"I used to, but since we moved, I haven't had the time to pick it up again. New school, new friends." He looked back at me. "But then, you know how that is, don't you?"

"Yeah. You have your sister, though, right?" I thought, kind of jealous. It would be a lot easier moving somewhere with a sibling.

Devon laughed, "Yeah, Dani. I love her, but she and I don't always see eye to eye." Then he turned serious. "Have you all talked anymore about the Daïmonids, and what you're going to do about them?"

I turned to my paperback of Romeo and Juliet and flipped through the pages. "No. I mean, Cole, as my Guardian, has been kind of leading the charge on that, and, well, he seems to be avoiding me lately. For some reason." I tried to keep the hurt out of my voice.

Wanting to change the subject, I looked up at Devon. "Did you ever find out anything about our rings? Or yours at least?" I asked curiously, turning my hand over and looking at the initials.

"Oh, yeah! My father said that both Dani's and my rings were the wedding rings of our great-great-grandparents, and the initials are theirs. He didn't think that they had any special powers, but my grandfather was kind of the black sheep in our family, so anything's possible." He grinned at me and twisted his own ring around his finger.

"I did find a book in our library that mentioned a few rings that were made a couple of centuries ago that were talismans in a ceremony. Do you know if yours could have been one of those rings?" He asked as he reached out with his hand and touched my ring. That same warm glow that we had felt before and a golden shimmer enveloped our hands.

I slipped mine away, feeling kind of guilty. I had asked Cole to the Sadie Hawkins dance, and I really liked him, so I didn't understand these new feelings I was having for Devon. I looked up at him and smiled slightly. "Let's get to work on our homework, Romeo."

Chapter 16

Devon

When I got home from the beach, thinking back on my conversation with Avery, I decided to dig around in the library and see if I could come up with any more information about the rings Dani and I had inherited.

I knocked on the library door, but when there was no answer, I opened it and stepped inside. I glanced around, noting that there wasn't anyone else here, and took a deep breath. There were windows that ran from floor to ceiling, interspersed throughout the room. The curtains had been drawn back so that light was shining brightly into the room. I could see dust floating and shimmering through the light.

I flashed back to the library we had in our house where I grew up, where my grandmother taught me how to use my Mesmer gifts. She had died a couple of years ago, but those were some of my favorite memories. She was very gentle, and her tone was always so soothing such a stark contrast to the brusqueness that my father displayed towards me my entire life. I shrugged off those bad memories and started looking through one of the bookshelves.

I thought I had left that old journal around here somewhere. The room brightened suddenly, and I noticed the dust start to swirl and form a wave, moving towards the other end of the room. The dust was lit up, like stars on a dark sky, and curious, I followed that wave until it stopped and hovered in front of a shelf. There were some old, thin leather-bound books with faded ink on the covers. I grabbed one and cracked it open, sinking into a chair behind me. *Gotcha*, I thought.

"The journal of Atticus Finn," a voice spoke from in front of me, and I jerked my head up in surprise. Standing in front of me, was a man, tall, with dark blonde hair and blue eyes. He was wearing loose brown pants and a white collared shirt with rolled up sleeves. The figure shimmered and I realized that I could see through him to the wall behind. I shut the book. The figure disappeared. I opened it again, and the figure appeared, stating quietly, "The journal of Atticus Finn."

"Cool!" I said quietly to myself. I sat there, waiting for who I assumed to be Atticus, to speak. Nothing. I looked down at the book, and realized that I was on the title page, which read, "The Journal of Atticus Finn." I turned the page, and the figure started speaking.

"May 13, 1816. Today, a few Committee members gathered together in the museum's basement. Flora and I, as well as Thomas Sullivan and Gaea Cleary had discovered some old documents that would support our theory about tying our powers together through focus objects. These documents were over a century old and had been written by scholars like us at the University of Essex. They told of failed experiments that caused deaths among the members who held them. There were many notations regarding each experiment, which looked to have been building up to a—" The figure in front of me paused, and I hurriedly turned the page. "—final act, which would entail calling forth and holding a Daïmon in a summoning circle. The plan was for the members of the circle to siphon the Daïmon's powers into a focus object, one for each member. The four of us were very excited. Flora, Gaea, and I wanted to hurry to complete the ritual, but Thomas, always playing devil's advocate, pointed out with caution that all but one of those members had died trying to complete this ritual."

I skimmed through the journal, ignoring the figure in front of me who seemed to flicker and start talking, depending upon how long I paused at a page. Suddenly, I came up with an idea.

"Atticus," I said to my great-great-grandfather.

"Yes?" he replied.

Huh, I thought to myself, *it worked!* "Atticus, skip to final ritual please."

The figure flickered and whirred, then stopped suddenly. "Volume 2, October 31, 1816. After Thomas backed out of the experiment, Flora, Gaea, and I decided we would move on with this journey ourselves. Tonight, Samhain, will be the most powerful time to be able to complete the ritual. We are calling forth the Avdar from his dimension Tolterell, and we will confine him to our circle. We are all using rings that we had made, each with our initials inscribed on them, to hold the power we will capture." Atticus held up his hand as he said this, giving me a clear look at the ring I now wore on my own hand. "This exercise will make Flora and I the most powerful Elemental members, attaining the status we had always wanted, and achieving immortality. We have never understood Gaea's reasons for joining us, as she doesn't seem to want the power, and is also a Seer, but we need a third to complete the Triad, and she seems willing."

Impatient with this monologue, I ask Atticus to skip to midnight, when the ritual occurred.

"October 31, 11:59 p.m. Flora, Gaea, and I have created a circle with salt that has been blessed by priests from our clan and are waiting for the clock to strike midnight. Our rings lay on a stone altar next to me, on our side of the circle. We have created an enchantment with our Elemental magic, and Gaea will start chanting the spell. We hear the church bells start to ring the first stroke of midnight. Log, set to record."

As I listen and watch Atticus speak, I am fiddling with the ring on my finger, in awe of what I am listening to. We learned of this in school, but I didn't realize that Dani's and my rings were those used in this famous ritual. Somehow Avery must be related to Gaea, and this is why our rings react to each other.

A more monotone voice speaks, and the figure of Atticus has frozen in front of me.

"*At the strike of twelve*
we, the Triad of Conn use our force of will
to call forth the Daïmon Avdar of Tolterell
and will siphon with this spell
his power into those objects shelved."

There is an explosive pop, and a loud roaring, which turns into an evil chuckle. Through this noise, I hear my great great-grandfather Atticus speaking over Gaea, who is continuing her chant.

"Avdar, you have been called forth and will feel our strength of will! Flora! Gaea! Join hands!"

The noise gets louder, and the growling wind grows stronger.

"With our names, Finn and Cleary, we unite and draw your power from you, using the powers of Earth, Fire, Air, and Water!" With the completion of those names, a shriek of rage howls through the room. Wind rips through the library, and then suddenly all is still. Papers flutter to the ground.

"Flora! Flora, answer me!" I hear Atticus yelling.

I jerked at the sound of a guttural voice that must be the Daïmon. "The names of Finn and Cleary will be remembered, and I vow to get back that which you have stolen from me!" With a loud crash, Avdar is gone.

I hear a quiet sobbing, and then the sound cuts off.

Sitting in the chair, I am struggling to breathe. I look at the ring on my hand, which had been throbbing with warmth during that final remembrance. I try to pull it off my hand, but it won't release my finger, and in fact, seems fused into my skin. I take note of the mess in the library, but ignore it all, to run out the front door, my heart racing. I need to talk to Avery about this right away—this explains what's been going on!

Chapter 17

Avery

I opened the door as Devon was about to knock on it. I had heard his Camaro drive up. That was fast! I stepped back to let him in through the store door. The shop was closed, but you could still smell the scent of mint and Earl Grey, and a hint of vanilla from the shortbread cookies Brenna had made to sell earlier.

He looked around curiously, and I could see him sniff, taking in the scent. He flashed a smile at me and raised a blonde brow in question.

"Um, our apartment is in the back, if you want to come in?" As I asked the question I saw him glance towards the back door. "My aunt is actually out on an errand, so no one is, um, here right now." I spoke tentatively, not entirely comfortable being alone with him at my house.

We walked into the kitchen and wanting something to do I opened the fridge. "Did you want a glass of iced tea or a soda?"

I poured us each a glass of tea and got some of my aunt's oatmeal cookies out of a jar and put them on a plate. After working in the shop, getting drinks and sweets or plating cookies was done out of habit. Devon seemed appreciative though, as he grabbed a cookie and his glass and headed over to the couch. He threw himself down and let out a big sigh, taking a big gulp of his tea.

"Okay, when I got home this afternoon, I decided to do some more research in our library." He paused to take a drink of his tea, and then proceeded to explain what he'd learned about his grandparents from the journal.

"I know your last name is Anderson, but Avery, have you ever heard the name Gaea Cleary before?" As he said that name, I glanced down at the initials on my ring. GC. I touched it gently, and then looked at his ring. AF.

"No, but my mom wasn't really into family history lessons. I didn't even know about my Aunt Brenna. However," I looked at him and glanced at my ring again, "my middle name is Cleary. Avery Cleary Anderson."

"Well, I think that says it all, don't you?" He said and looked meaningfully at my ring and then put his hand in the air to show me his. "You have to be her relative if her ring is passed down in your family, just like mine is."

"But, when Cole and Brenna told me about my background, they didn't mention anything about her, other than that she and Atticus called forth the Daïmon." Shocked, I got up and sat back down again.

"It's possible that she doesn't know." At my look of confusion, he clarified. "If the ring is passed down from mother to first born daughter, then your own mother would have gotten the ring from your grandmother, and the story with it. She gave it to you right before she died, right?" I nodded a yes.

"Like, literally, a couple weeks before," I said quietly remembering that moment. "But she didn't tell me anything about it!" I said in frustration.

"She may have meant to tell you, but just ran out of time," he said gently, and I nodded my agreement.

"Okay, so what does this mean?" I asked in confusion.

"With the attacks increasing from the Daïmonids, we know they think you will have the power to send Avdar back to his dimension, Tolterell."

"Which is why they want to get rid of me," I stated.

"Uh, yeah," he said, nodding his head emphatically.

"But, you and Dani have the other rings. So...," I trailed off not really knowing what the significance was.

"Yeah. Well, we know the rings work together because we won that fight against the Daïmonids by joining our powers." He looked at me. "But, they can also be used against each other, like when you and Dani shook hands in biology class and the place kind of exploded."

"I guess we need to be careful until we can figure out what to do." I looked past his shoulder out the window and noticed that clouds had covered the sun, and it had turned into a gloomy day just like my mood.

"Yeah, I guess so," he agreed. "Have you noticed what the day is today?" I looked back at him.

"I know, Samhain is next Saturday. And, um, my birthday is also on Halloween."

He raised his eyebrows at me and said, "This should be an interesting week."

The following day the conversations at school all concerned the dance. The conversations among my friends all centered around my sixteenth birthday, and my growing powers. Cole, after a couple of days of missing school, returned to our group as if nothing had happened. Distracted by my growing friendship with Devon I didn't press him about his absence. He and I got in a couple of practice sessions in between our games, homework, and my job at the tea shop, but I didn't really learn anything new. Summer and Ben often hung out with us during those sessions, and Ana also dropped in occasionally around her party decorating schedule.

We were all together this afternoon in my aunt's backyard. Cole and I just finished today's training, which was really just improving what I'd already learned. With practice, I could fling bolts of energy pretty quickly, and also cast a shield around myself and anyone standing near me. Summer had been a great help, using herself as a moving target. I was worried about hurting her, but Cole explained to me that my intent had to be to harm in order for my bolt to have that kind of power. So, since I didn't want to hurt her, my bolt just gave her a slight zap. She was so quick that I only hit her with a bolt once, and when I did she giggled, saying that it tickled.

We were relaxing around the table drinking iced tea and eating some shortbread cookies. I was tired of everyone's focus being on me so I deflected that attention to Ana.

"Ana, how's the decorating going for the dance? You should be about finished with the dance being this weekend, right?" I asked quickly, before someone could bring up practicing another round of flinging bolts or hurling clods of dirt.

Everyone looked at Ana, who flushed from her natural peachy skin tone, her freckles twirling wildly. Her natural instinct to turn her skin the shade behind her, which was the white wall of the house. Interestingly enough, white didn't seem to be a color that her skin could turn. Her freckles slowed down and her skin turned back to her natural shade. The wind blew a piece of hair across her nose and she reached out to push it behind her ear.

She gave a Mona Lisa smile, "We are pretty much finished." She had been pretty quiet about the decorations for the party, and there seemed to be a vow of silence among the committee members. She had however, mentioned last week that Dani was drafted to the committee by a couple of her new cheerleader friends.

"What about Dani, is she still ignoring you?" I asked curiously. We hadn't seen a lot of her lately and only noticed her lurking about a couple of times.

"Well, she isn't so much ignoring me as not noticing when I'm around," she said with a small smile." She is very busy cementing her status with the cheerleaders, and none of them really pay much attention to me."

Dani had her tryouts with the cheerleading squad and had easily made the team. Apparently, the gossip we had heard in class when she had first started was true. She was a really gifted gymnast, and the squad had already shown her off at her first football game. I'd heard that when our team had scored the winning touchdown she'd done front walkovers all the way down the football field, ending with a back flip.

"One of the girls asked about Devon, trying to find out if he had a girlfriend, I guess. She said that he was already interested in someone here at school, so not to get her hopes up." Summer, Ana, and I exchanged a look. Cole and Ben didn't know this, but Devon and I had met almost every day to memorize our scene from Romeo and Juliet. He was still asking about Cole and me, especially since Cole had returned to the group. I've told him we weren't a couple, and in fact, Cole wasn't acting interested at all, which was kind of confusing. When Devon asked who I was going to the dance with, and I said Cole, he just grinned and said, "Thought so." The second time Devon brought him up, he told me that since Cole and I weren't a couple, he was going to go stag to the dance and he hoped to see me there. With mixed feelings I told him that I'm sure there were several girls who would be happy to go with him, and he said he'd been asked, and had turned everyone down which I have to admit made me kind of happy.

I am so messed up. I mean, I really liked Cole, but it seemed like he was conflicted about being my Guardian and well, anything else. After spending some time with Devon, he didn't seem as strange as he first had, and actually, he was kind of growing on me, becoming a friend.

Summer opened her mouth, and I hurried to interrupt her. "Summer, have you finally decided what costumes you and Ben are going to wear to the dance?" This easily distracted her, as our costumes had been a hot topic last week at lunch. All of the couples going to the dance were dressing as famous pairs from history or Hollywood.

"Well, Ben and I are going to go as Marilyn Monroe and JFK." I could easily see Summer in that iconic white dress.

"So, that means Bens costume is just wearing a suit?"

"You'll just have to wait and see, won't you?" Ben wiggled his eyebrows at me and I laughed. "Have you two decided who you are going as?"

Cole quirked his eyebrow at me, his piercing glinting in the sunlight. I laughed, "We're going as Bella and Edward." I had seen every *Twilight* movie and thought Cole would make a hot vampire.

"Before or after she turns vampy?" Ana asked.

"I thought I'd surprise you guys." I had bought some white iridescent makeup that would help out with Cole's vampire glow. The four of us made plans to drive together to the dance. Ana, who was working the refreshment table, was going to meet us there and I never even thought to ask if she had a date.

Chapter 18

Devon

I parked my car next to my sister's Jeep in the driveway. Finally! She'd been avoiding me, and I've wanted to talk to her about what she was doing on that building when we got attacked by those Daïmonids!

The door to her room was open, so I let myself in. "Hi." I leaned against the door jamb, watching her put makeup on at her desk. She looked at me in the mirror with a glint in her eye.

"Hey." She went back to putting on her mascara.

"So, I see you've met a few scary friends lately," I said watching her closely for a reaction.

She sighed, "They aren't my friends, but they are our father's associates." She turned around in her seat to face me a strange look on her face.

I straightened away from the door. "What?" I spoke rather loudly, and she shushed me and motioned for me to close the door.

I shut the door and turned to face her. "Why would our Father be associating with Daïmonids?" I took a step towards her, but she stood up and I stopped.

"Come on, Devon, don't be an idiot!" She flashed her hand at me, showing her ring, an exact duplicate of mine.

"When father gave us these rings, he said that one day we would be using them." She flung her hair over her shoulder.

"You've been so busy playing nice with Avery that you've forgotten the reason why we were put into the same school with her!" She angrily walked over to her bed and picked up her purse. She threw the strap onto her shoulder and turned around.

"Father has told me the real reason why we are here, because he knew you wouldn't be able to handle it." She said pointing a finger at me.

"Okay, I'll play, why are we really here?" I asked, even though I could see where this conversation was going and I did not like it.

"Avery, on her sixteenth birthday, is going to develop her powers, both Elemental and Seer, and you are going to take them from her. With my help." She gestured at our rings. "These rings will enable us to draw her power from her. You've felt how they react to her!"

"Yes, and I've also seen how her ring reacts to us." I looked at her in question. "Why would you think that this wouldn't backfire on us? She may be able to take our powers, too?" I looked at Dani and sat down in the seat she had vacated at her desk. "I suppose father told you how we were going to be able to do this?"

"Yes, he did." Dani's expression showed her nervous excitement. "We are going to be there when she inherits her powers, during her transition." She laughed, "I can't wait to see the look on her face when we strip them from her!"

"And the Daïmonids?" I couldn't figure out why they would let us be strong enough to vanquish Avdar. "What do they get out of this?"

"Avdar, needs a mortal vessel. Once you and I have taken Avery's powers, he will inhabit your body. You will rule!" Her eyes glowed with an insane light.

My family is crazy, I thought, shocked by the idea. I nodded my head, playing along "Okay, so we are NOT going to vanquish him, we are going to let Avdar have my body, and wreak havoc on our world?" I tried to keep the horror from showing, hoping my face was as blank as my voice.

"Yes!" She ran towards me and gave me a huge hug. "Isn't this fabulous! Our family will be the ultimate power!" I lightly hugged her, and awkwardly gave her a pat on the back. Having delivered her news, Dani took off out of the room. My sister is officially insane!

"Yeah, go us." Like I'm going to sacrifice myself so a Daïmon can wipe us all out? Not if I can help it.

That morning, our class was meeting in the auditorium. I tapped my foot nervously against the floor and looked around for Avery. She wasn't usually late for class, and the second pair was already on the stage. We had been practicing almost every evening for the last few days in preparation for our scene. I was pulling my beaten up copy of Romeo and Juliet out of my backpack when the door slammed behind me. I whipped my head around and breathed a sigh of relief. Avery, Cole, and Ana walked in together. Avery hurried over to the seat next to me and slid into it. I looked behind her at Cole, and saw his face set angrily. *It seems like that's the only face the guy puts on anymore*, I thought.

"What's going on? I didn't think you were going to make it." I leaned towards her and whispered in her ear. I saw her shoulder move up a fraction, as she shivered slightly.

The smell of grass and lemon lingered. I took a breath, savoring her scent.

"Cole. He's just, well, he isn't really happy with this assignment." She said and I glanced at Cole, sitting two rows back and smirked at him. He frowned back at me.

"No kidding. Well, put that out of your head." I nodded towards our teacher. "Newsome has put up the list, and we are going third."

"Great." Avery said wrapping her arms around herself and nervously looked at the stage where two of our classmates were butchering the fight scene from the beginning of the book.

"Hey," I tipped her chin towards me so that our eyes met, "we can't be any worse than them, right?" As I said that, the sound of swords clashing and two guys stiltedly saying their lines made her smile.

"Yeah, you're right. I just, well, I haven't done anything like this before." She said as she reached out and touched my arm and I stared down at her hand in shock. She'd never touched me on her own before.

I covered her hand with mine, and our rings started to warm up, and a little sizzle went through me. She jumped slightly, so I knew that she felt it as well.

We jerked apart at the sound of clapping and looked around. The two idiots on stage took bows and clapped each other on the shoulders. Mr. Newsome took their props away from them and set them aside, then looked at his clipboard.

"Avery, Devon, you're up!" Newsome yelled, and I stood and wiped my hands nervously on my jeans, then offered a hand to Avery to help her up. I heard some light applause and saw Summer slip into her seat beside Ana. They both were clapping and giving us encouragement. Avery smiled shyly over at them.

"Let's do this!" I said putting out my fist for her to bump lightly, and we headed for the stage.

We had decided to start in the middle of one of the scenes, skipping Juliet's monologue and jumping right into their interaction. Avery headed across the stage and turned around to stare blankly at the audience. I stayed across the stage, to her right, waiting.

She closed her eyes and took a deep breath. As she did this, her hair started to move gently, and a soft glow lit her features.

"Romeo.

'Tis but thy name that is my enemy." Avery's eyes opened and she looked directly at me, her hazel eyes had turned green and glowed. Immediately entranced, I took a step towards her as she continued to speak.

"Though art thyself, though not a Montague. What's a Montague? It is no hand, nor foot, nor arm, nor face, nor any other part belonging to a man." She reached up and pushed a wavering strand of hair behind her ear. "O, be some other name! What's in a name?"

I stepped closer, and as I started to respond, I noticed the light that lit her reached out towards me and engulfed me in its embrace as well. I reached my hand towards her, my ring glittering in the light. "I take thee at thy word. Call me but love, and I'll be new baptized. Henceforth, I will never be Romeo."

As we continued through the short scene, I reflected upon these words, again, and how this situation was about what other people wanted, and not what I wanted or what was good for me, a kind of familiar theme in my life right now. I looked at Avery, who was looking earnestly at me as she quoted her last line, "Art thou not Romeo, and a Montague?"

As I started to say my last line, I felt a click, and our energy snapped together, which turned the light a soft pale blue color, "Neither, fair maid, if either you dislike." I quoted softly, meaning every word.

The sound of loud applause and a few whistles broke the spell that Avery and I had woven with each other. I blinked and then gave her a grin, and she smiled proudly back. I took her hand and we bowed to the audience. I could hear Summer yell, "Way to go, Avery!" I laughed and looked over at her to see she was blushing slightly but she looked pleased.

I heard Newsome say something about the lighting, and noticed him looking at the darkness in the back of the auditorium and the lack of a lighting tech. He frowned slightly in confusion and then shrugged.

There was a door off to the side of the stage and we left through that door, as did the performers before us, so that we could enter the auditorium from the back again, but I stopped Avery before we took more than a few steps. I felt a rush of energy pulse through me and grabbed her for a hug. She laughed and lightly hugged me back.

"That was awesome!" I tightened my arms around her and then quickly released her. She looked up at me with a grin.

"That went better than I thought it would."

"You were in the zone, and that lighting was brilliant!" I exclaimed noticing her blush slightly.

"Well, that was kind of an accident, but I've been practicing meditation, and sometimes, I, uh, start to glow." She looked down at her feet but then peeked up at me through her hair. "It didn't seem like such a bad thing it happened this time."

"Absolutely! We killed it! Though, I think Newsome was a bit confused, but he'll get over it." I grabbed her hand

and started walking rapidly down the hall but stopped when I felt her pull on my hand.

"Um, we just passed the door?" She said giving me a questioning look.

"Yeah, we aren't sticking around to hear everyone else, cause they are all going to suck in comparison. Let's go somewhere and celebrate!" I said, laughing.

"I should really be in there for Cole and Ana's." I heard her say, but I ignored her and grabbed her hand and started hauling her out to my car.

Chapter 19

Cole

This is torture, I thought, as I watched Avery laugh at something Summer said. Ben's antics since he and Summer were now an item seemed to have worsened. He was always trying to make her laugh, because she'd giggle and then nudge her head against his chest. I looked back at Avery again, and saw her looking across the quad. I followed her gaze and saw Devon sitting alone under a tree.

After Avery and Devon's performance on stage the other day, I could tell that creepy tension had turned into something else. It had been hard to go on stage with Ana and quote our scene because I'd kept glancing towards the back of the auditorium waiting for Avery to come back in the room. As our scene disintegrated, Ana had just faded until her voice was the only piece of her present in the room. Needless to say, we hadn't gotten a very good grade.

I glared hard at Devon, then caught myself. Why did I even care if I was going to follow my orders? I stiffened when I saw him smirk my way and made myself relax. I looked back towards Ben and Summer again to break eye contact.

The sun was shining brightly, glinting in Avery's dark blonde hair as she took her sandwich out of the wrapper.

Why couldn't she have been just a normal girl? She looked at me and nodded at her sandwich, asking if I'd like half. I shook my head and looked away. I noticed a bird fly across the sky behind her and land in the tree over our heads. A blackbird with red stripes on its wings cocked its head and looked from Avery to me.

I took a deep breath. Was this the Sentinel, checking in on his daughter? Or just a blackbird? It trilled softly, then flew off again, and I breathed a little easier. Avery's birthday was Saturday night, and she'd start to gain more powers at the stroke of midnight.

The sound of paper caught my attention and I saw Ana hand Avery and Summer a flyer for the dance. It was Friday night, and despite everything, I really wanted Avery to have a good time. After all that night could be her last.

Last night when I got home, my dad was in his office talking on the phone. He didn't know I was home yet, and he was arguing heatedly with Mathis on the phone. I heard my name mentioned and I crept closer to the door. My father was assuring Mathis that I was on board with the mission, but I could hear the doubt in his voice. He asked Mathis if that seat on the Committee that he'd given up when we moved here was still open. I could hear the relief in his voice. Thinking of all that my father had given up for this mission, his place on the Committee and the honor that comes with that position. My shoulders slumped slightly. I didn't want to disappoint him! I touched the bar in my eyebrow, the power tingling through my finger giving me confidence. I squeezed my eyes shut then opened them to look at Avery laughing with her friends. I straightened my shoulders with resolve and pushed my feelings into a dark corner of my heart.

Chapter 20

Avery

When the four of us walked through the doors of the gym, we stopped to take in the transformation. The bench seats that normally lined the wall were pushed back leaving only one row to sit on. Bales of hay were piled in each corner of the room to create seating areas for the students. Orange and black twinkly lights were strung across the top of the room and fog was drifting across a dance floor already filled with students moving to the music of the DJ set up on the stage. Jack-o-lanterns lined the edge of the stage. Some of their faces set in scary grimaces, while others were more comical.

I noticed a refreshment table set up across the room and looked around for Ana. I watched a girl step up to the table and jumped slightly when Ana materialized in front of her. Ana was wearing black leggings and a black cotton turtleneck. Her hair was pulled back in a ponytail, leaving her bangs to frame her small pointed face. I think she was dressed up as Audrey Hepburn, from an American in Paris' beatnik scene. I could tell she was having fun, her skin glowed a soft peach tint.

A flash of light caught my attention and I looked over to the left of the door at a photographer taking pictures of couples arranged in front of a backdrop with a huge full moon and a witch flying on a broom in silhouette.

"Let's take pictures!" Summer grabbed my hand and ran over to the photographer, Ben and Cole following behind us. A couple finished taking their picture and the four of us stepped in front of the camera. Ben grabbed Summer and held her in front of him, but slightly to the side since he was a couple inches shorter. Summer looked beautiful in her white Marilyn Monroe dress. Her hair was done in a loose curly style very reminiscent of the 60s. Ben was wearing a suit, but his blonde hair was slicked back and styled to look somewhat like JFK's did when he was the president. He was wearing a sash across his chest, kind of like Miss America's, but his read: Happy Birthday Mr. President.

When Cole had shown up at my house, he was dressed in a black suit with a white shirt and black tie. He wore some black eyeliner and gelled his hair so that it looked a little messier than normal. He had liberally dusted his face with the iridescent powder I had bought earlier that week.

When I looked over to him as we stepped in front of the camera, it was hard not to notice how cute he was, his purple eyes were even more defined from the eyeliner he was wearing. He was still wearing his eyebrow piercing, even though Edward never had one in the movies. My costume was pretty easy since Bella Swann was not a fancy dresser. She wore jeans, t-shirt and a hoodie in most scenes, which I thought was kind of boring. So, I decided that we were going to be Bella and Edward at their wedding. Ana and I had gone out to a second-hand store and I found a wedding dress that only had a couple of tears along the hem. Cole and I both wore wedding rings, and I held a fake bouquet of flowers. I had colored my two-toned hair a soft one toned brown. I hoped the color rinsed out after one washing, like it was supposed to.

Cole reached for my hand and pulled me in front of him. I stood there wondering what was running through his head, the Cole that I had met a month ago had disappeared, and this cool, kind of angry Cole stood in his place. I looked at Summer and Ben, mugging for the camera. She had the front of her dress held down just like in that famous pose of Marilyn on the subway grate, while Ben was standing at her side with a cheesy grin on his face and his hand sliding up her leg, pushing her dress up. Cole moved my hair off my neck and I felt his breath on my skin and a couple of pricks from his fake vampire teeth surprised a shiver out of me. Just as that shiver ran through me, the light flashed from the camera. Summer and Ben laughed and walked away so the next couple could have their picture taken, but Cole grabbed my hand and held me still for a moment. Confused, I looked up at him.

"You okay?" He asked cocking his eyebrow at me. He gave me a soft smile, and again it was like a switch was thrown, and the old Cole was back. I looked down at his hand holding mine, embarrassed that he had felt that shiver, and nodded.

"Sure. Um, are you okay?" I asked, trying to read his mind. He gave me a blank stare then smiled slightly and nodded. We followed Summer and Ben over to the refreshment table, and when I tried to release his hand, he firmly gripped mine and linked our fingers. Surprised, I gave his hand a squeeze and left mine in his content to keep the peace for the moment.

Ana materialized as we approached the table. I saw her take note of Cole holding my hand and she raised an eyebrow at me. I shrugged with a "Your guess is as good as mine" look, but smiled. She smiled back, pleased to see it.

"Audrey Hepburn, right?" I said, gesturing with my hand towards her outfit. "All you're missing is Fred Astaire."

"Oh." She said quickly, "He's here somewhere!" Summer and I exchanged looks. As far as we knew, Ana had come to the dance by herself.

Ana looked over her shoulder and gestured. A tall skinny boy I had not noticed stepped away from the wall and came up behind Ana. He was also wearing black leggings and a black button-down shirt, but he had a scarf tied around his neck.

"This is my friend, Stick." Stick nodded and blended back into the wall. "Stick is the son of a friend of my fathers." She whispered urgently. "Daddy wouldn't let me come to the dance by myself, even though I didn't want a date." I could tell she was upset because the freckles on her skin were whirling madly. Ana threw a frustrated look over her shoulder.

"Let me know if you need me to run interference." Summer whispered back to her. We both looked over Ana's shoulder and tried to spot Stick against the wall. Chameleons were hard to notice anyway but put them in black clothing in a dark room, and well, they were pretty invisible unless they wanted to be seen.

"Oh. He's all right." Ana took a breath and let it out gently. "Daddy frustrates me more than anything. You'd think I lived in the Middle Ages or something."

Summer and I exchanged a look. I had told her about the conversation Ana and I had about her father. He was a little eccentric, living in a bunker behind the house Ana lived in with her aunt. A little overprotective, he would sometimes overreact, and it seemed that this was one of those times.

I reached out a hand to Ana, in sympathy, but she brushed me off, changing the subject.

"I'm glad you and Cole are together tonight. I meant to tell you," Ana's sentence trailed off.

"Tell me?" I whispered back to her. Summer leaned in to hear better.

"I had told you that I would try to find out why he was acting so strange over the last week?" She whispered, looking over our shoulders at Ben and Cole who were standing with their backs to us, watching the dance floor.

"I, um, overheard him talking on his cell phone to his dad yesterday." She looked at us with a confused expression on her face.

"Yeah?" I whispered to her, to hurry her along.

"He, was, umm, in the boy's locker room, after soccer practice." At this, Summer and I exchanged glances with raised eyebrows.

"Sugar, do tell!" Summer grinned at her.

I laughed and thought that some of those training exercises her dad had her doing must have come in handy.

Ana blushed a becoming shade of pink, her freckles swirling wildly. "Oh hush. I was trying to not be seen!"

I can imagine, I thought. *Her specialty is blending in to the background.*

We all looked around at raised voices behind us to see Ben joking around with Cole and I gestured for her to continue.

"He was having an argument with his Dad. I didn't catch all of it, but it was about you, Avery. Your birthday tomorrow night?" I nodded at her. "His dad is telling him to do something before your birthday."

"Maybe buy her a great gift?" Summer joked.

"Um, I don't think so? I mean, Cole was pretty angry. Saying that he said he'd do it, and he could stop checking in with him about it. That's all I could hear though." She looked down in embarrassment.

"Hey, thanks, it's nice to know you have my back." I touched her hand gently, wondering what Cole was supposed to be doing. I looked over at him, but out of the darkness a glass full of punch was thrust forward to me and I found myself taking it. Stick was suddenly standing next to Ana. He poured Summer a glass as well.

"Um, thanks Stick," Summer said raising the glass to her lips and taking a sip.

"No problem," he replied, taking a step backwards again. I took a drink of my punch. Not bad, it didn't taste like anyone had spiked it yet, and truly, with Stick and Ana standing guard unseen, I doubt anyone would.

Ben called to Summer and me, "Come on ladies, I love this song, it's a classic!" He grabbed Summer's hand and she grabbed mine. I looked at Cole as I was being dragged towards the dance floor. He scooped the cup out of my hand, drained it and followed.

We hit the dance floor and started dancing to some 80s song I'd never heard of called, appropriately, "Dead Man's Party." Ben loved 80s music and he said it was by some band called Oingo Boingo. Weird name, but Ben was right, the song was awesome!

As the four of us danced, I took a look at the couples around us. Dancing among us were the couple from the dance poster Elvis and Priscilla Presley. Next to them Barack and Michelle Obama, and Mr. and Mrs. Brady in 70s outfits. You could tell the drama department really got into this because there were some really great costumes. Elizabeth Taylor as Cleopatra, with some guy dressed in a Gladiator outfit, Lucille Ball had a huge red wig wearing a house dress and Desi Arnaz was carrying a set of bongos, and two guys were dressed as the Lone Ranger and Tonto. I raised a brow. *Cool*, I thought.

The song ended and a slow song started up. Summer and Ben immediately cuddled up swaying to the music. I sighed and turned to walk off the dance floor and was surprised when Cole caught my arm. I glanced up and noticed he was looking at me intently. I raised an eyebrow in question.

"Avery, let's stay and dance." He said quietly, tugging me towards him. Kind of weirded out but also kind of happy that sweet Cole was back I allowed myself to be pulled to him, my arms trapped between us. I'd never slow danced with anyone before tonight, so I wasn't sure what I was supposed to do with my arms. Embarrased, I looked over at Summer and noticed that she had her arms slung over Ben's shoulders, so I pushed my hands up Cole's chest until they reached his neck. I looked up, caught him looking down at me, and I raised an eyebrow back at him then put my cheek on his chest and closed my eyes. I felt his arms tighten a little bit, and I relaxed slowly as we swayed from side to side, his chin settled on the top of my head.

"I'm going to stay in my car outside your house tomorrow night." Cole said to the top of my head.

"What? Why?" Confused with his comment, I lifted my head off his chest and looked at him.

"You turn sixteen at the stroke of midnight." I felt him playing with the bottom of my hair in the middle of my back, and then his hands splayed protectively over me. "I want to make sure everything goes well for you."

It might be overkill to have Cole sitting outside in a car, but it did make me feel slightly better knowing that if something were to happen, I wouldn't be alone.

Just as I started to nod in agreement, the DJ changed speed and started a fast song again. The four of us started dancing, and I felt a nudge on my right hand side. I smiled at Ana, as she and Stick joined us. The six of us moved among each other changing partners, until I was dancing opposite Stick. He was very tall, probably 6′1″, and skinny, compared to Ana's 5′1″, but I noticed that even though he was paired up with me, his eyes remained on Ana. I followed his gaze and noticed that she and Ben were laughing. Ben twirled her around and her hair flew around her face, her skin a soft peach tone that told me she was happy. She looked beautiful. I looked back at Stick. He definitely thought so too. He couldn't take his eyes off her.

Cole and Summer were dancing together, with Summer talking his ear off and making him laugh. Just as I was about to edge Stick towards them, my arm was grabbed from behind and I was spun in a different direction. I twirled around a couple of times laughing and then came to a stop facing Devon. He had spun me away from my friends, to the edge of the dance floor. The cheerleading squad, led by Dani, danced between my friends and me. I could just see the top of Cole's head as he danced with Summer, and Stick hadn't known I was gone, as he was still looking towards Ana.

Devon, wearing a white suit with angel's wings, was moving in front of me, dancing to the quick beat in the song. I glanced over to my friends who hadn't even noticed I was gone, so I started moving to the music as well. *One dance with Devon wouldn't hurt anyone*, I thought, kind of happy that he didn't ask in front of Cole. He seemed pleased that I stayed with him and he smiled at me, his blue eyes lightening and the pupils almost disappearing. I shivered knowing Cole would be angry, and he rubbed his hands up and down my arms.

"Where's your date?" I asked him, taking his hands off my arms and looking around, curiously.

"The girl I wanted to bring to this dance already had a date, so I came stag." He swung around me so that when I was facing him, my back was to my friends. He pointed at me. "In case you hadn't figured it out that girl was you."

I smiled uncomfortably. I was conflicted by my feelings for both Devon and Cole. Both of them were acting differently than they had a couple of weeks ago. It was like they had switched bodies. Devon seemed nice and well, things with Cole had gotten kind of weird. The music ended and I knew my friends were going to figure out that I wasn't with them and I didn't want to cause any problems tonight between Devon and Cole.

"Well, I'm glad we got to dance, but I don't want to be rude to my date, and I need to get back to my friends." I turned away from him, hoping to escape into the crowd, but he grabbed my elbow again. As he turned me around, the next song started up, and it was a slow song.

"Just one more dance," he said. "I have something I wanted to tell you." Behind me I heard a disturbance, and I knew Cole had figured out that I wasn't with their group. Devon looking over my shoulder saw this as well, but the cheerleaders were still separating me from my friends. They, with their dates, had created a blockade, so I wasn't really visible, yet. As he reached out to pull me to him again, the light flashed on his ring. I hesitated, but then gave in.

"Okay, one more dance," I said. "Did you find out anything else out about our rings?" I could feel my knees trembling slightly as I smiled at him. I stepped forward into his embrace.

"Funny," he said. "That's what I wanted to talk to you about." He hooked me around the waist with his left hand, pulling me into his arms. He brought his right hand up in front of my face.

"Hold it still. I want to compare them again." His hand stilled and I could see the initials scrolled across a silver shield. I held up my right hand, making sure not to touch his, and looked at my ring. Once again, I marveled at the fact that we both had these rings. My hand, beside his, was small and trembled slightly.

"Hey, careful Avery, I don't want to." He looked behind me and his hold tightened.

"To what?" I looked up at him in question and just as I put my hand on his waist I felt the air stir and I was suddenly out of Devon's arms, my back against Cole's chest. As he wrapped one arm across my shoulders and tucked me into his side, a breeze whipped Devon's hair around his head.

"I'm fine!" I said to Cole, struggling to get out from under his arm, but I found that my legs wouldn't obey me and felt like they were stuck to the floor. I looked to the side and could see Ben and Stick flanking Cole, with Summer and Ana standing behind them.

Devon, looking a little uncomfortable, laughed lightly, trying to make a joke out of it. "It was only a dance, and we were about to move back in your direction," he said, making a placating gesture. Cole gave me an inquiring look.

Confused, I tried to focus but my mind was fuzzy. I couldn't make sense of what was happening and I mumbled, "his ring." Devon lifted his hand in front of his body, looking down at his ring. The light glinted off the ring again. As it did, I found that I couldn't take my eyes off it.

"Come on, man, it was just a dance, and you interrupted our conversation. I'll make sure she's safe, promise." Devon held the hand with the ring out to me. Cole's arm tightened around my waist. I couldn't look away from his hand and I really wanted to reach out and take hold of it. I tried to move my arm again but couldn't. The air between Devon and me shimmered with a golden light. From far away, I could hear Summer saying my name and Cole took a step back dragging me with him. He reached up and took a hold of my chin and forced my eyes away from the ring. The light disappeared and I was staring into Cole's purple eyes.

Cole turned me away from Devon, calling Summer and Ana over and they each grabbed one of my hands. Cole turned back to Devon and took a step forward into his space. His hands were clenched into fists at his sides as he stared angrily at him. Ben stepped up behind Cole, put a hand on his shoulder and whispered into his ear. Cole nodded once and then turned away from Devon, following Ben back to where we were standing.

Concerned, Devon tried to keep walking beside me, trying to get my attention. "Avery, that shouldn't have happened, I think that it's our rings reacting to each other again." He looked into my eyes and frowned a bit, then looked at Cole. "It was an accident, let me talk to her one more time."

"No!" Cole said over his shoulder. He grabbed my hand away from Summer and we pushed through the mob of cheerleaders towards the other side of the gym. I stumbled a few times, my mind still unfocused. I could picture that ring, and the light it created. Hazily, I glanced over my shoulder towards him and saw that he hadn't moved. He was staring at me, with a sad look on his face, while his left hand twisted that ring around on his finger.

When I looked forward, I found we were at the punch bowl. Ana held out a glass of punch to me and as I was reaching to take it, I noticed my hand trembling. I pulled my hand away before I took the glass and reached up to push my hair away from my face. I shivered and rubbed my arms for warmth. I felt Cole step up so his front was against my back and I leaned into his warmth. He took the glass from Ana and brought it up to my mouth.

"Go ahead and take a drink. The sugar will help you come out from under his spell," he said quietly into my ear. I took a quick drink.

"Spell?" I must've said it kind of loud because I heard both Summer and Ana echo the word. "I was under a spell?"

"Yes, Devon must be a Mesmer, because I could feel you straining towards him, and when I looked into your eyes, they were blank and your pupils were dilated." Cole was talking loud enough for our group to hear him.

"A Mesmer has some sort of powers of hypnosis?" I was horrified that someone could have that kind of power over me and so easily. "That makes sense. I could hear all of you, but my body wasn't doing what I wanted it to." I turned around and gave Cole a grateful hug. I looked at my friends and wondered why Devon had tried to hypnotize me tonight, when I had been alone with him a lot over the past week and he hadn't tried it before? "Sugar, we'll always have your back." Summer grinned and tried to lighten the mood by saying, "I do want to hear more about Devon being a Mesmer, but not tonight. Come on guys, this is a dance, don't let that spoil our fun, let's dance!" She grabbed Ben, and after a nod from Cole, they moved out to the dance floor. Ana quietly stated that she was going to stay at the refreshment table, and Stick nodded that he was going to as well.

Thinking that it was probably a good idea to push what just happened aside to examine later, I looked at Cole as a slow song started playing. Choosing to brave the rejection, I asked. "Do you want to dance?" He looked conflicted, glancing back at Devon one more time, but he nodded, grabbed my hand, and led me out to the dance floor.

Chapter 21

Devon

I leaned back against the bleachers and looked down at my ring again. I didn't understand it; it takes intent to hypnotize or mesmerize someone, and I hadn't even tried to. I saw a pair of pink pumps stop in front of me and I looked up. Dani stood there in her 80s Madonna dress, black crinoline skirt and black bra under a white tank top.

"You need to stop moping around!" she hissed at me. "That was the perfect opportunity for you to gain control and make our jobs easier tomorrow night!"

I sighed. My sister had been pestering me lately with her plans to steal Avery's powers. I tried to play along, because it was better to know her plans, but I was almost positive that I wasn't going to help her do that. With the exception of tonight, I felt like our rings, Avery's and mine, would work together, and maybe it wasn't necessary to steal her powers from her. I shuddered lightly at the thought of being without my own powers.

I have heard what happens when Elementals lose their powers: they go insane and have to either be put in a facility or be put down like rabid dogs. It hasn't happened lately, but it used to be that when a crime was committed that was so heinous, like murder, that was their punishment. Murder was very rare in our society because of this.

Dani stood in front of me impatiently tapping her toe. "If you're done here, we have a meeting downtown with our father to make plans for tomorrow. I'm assuming since you came stag, you can go?" She turned around without waiting for an answer and I wondered, knowing that she hadn't come stag, how she was going to explain leaving the dance to her date.

I stood and gazed across the room at where Avery and her friends were dancing and laughing. I wished that she and I had more time together tonight. I saw her glance my way and I gave her a nod, then turned and left the building.

We parked in front of the same abandoned building as before and entered. I sensed men standing on the surrounding rooftops but couldn't see them very clearly.

As we entered the room, I saw my father sitting in a chair facing the door. He was talking to another man, whose back faced us. A fire was burning in the fireplace next to them. They both stood up when Dani and I walked in. My father nervously clasped his hands in front of him and stepped towards us.

"Devon, Dani, great, I'm glad you're here." As my father spoke the other man turned slowly around. He seemed to be around my father's age, with close cut brown hair, peppered with grey at the temples. He was wearing a pair of glasses that were tinted red, so I couldn't see his eye color very clearly. He did have on the familiar white button down and black slacks, which gave me a clue to his identity. I watched my sister as she moved eagerly forward.

"Dad! Is this him?" She was still dressed in her costume, although she had removed all of the excessive jewelry. She looked ridiculous next to their plain clothes.

"Dani, Devon, yes, this is Avdar." As my father spoke, Avdar walked forward, completely ignoring my sister, until he stopped in front of me. He circled around me, making me feel like he was checking out a horse to purchase.

I gave my father a hard stare and then turned around to face Avdar. "Would you like me to show you my teeth, as well?" I clenched my hands at my side, my teeth gritted in anger.

"Not necessary, I'm sure. Julian has kept me informed on your progress and health." Avdar gave my father a pleased nod and my father straightened his shoulders with pride.

At seeing my father's reaction, I incredulously realized that what Dani had told me was actually true. My father was planning to give my body and soul to Avdar. Lashing out, I shot a pulse of wind at my father, making him take a step back.

Seeing this, Avdar frowned, lifting a hand. Daïmonids stepped out of the shadows from each corner of the room. Dani stepped up next to me and put her hand on my arm trying to calm me, but I shrugged her off and stepped forward, getting into Avdar's space.

"This isn't going to happen," I stated, pointing first at him and then me. The wind that had been slowly circling through the room became a small whirlwind of anger, dancing next to me, and the fire grew into leaping flames in the fireplace. I saw Avdar look towards it and smile.

"Son, you don't want to test me. I may not be at full strength right now, but you are outnumbered here, and you will obey!" With the word obey, a lightning bolt crashed into the room, setting the blinds on the windows rattling. He removed his glasses, and I saw his pupils were an orange red color that grew brighter the longer I stared into them.

I was not going to just give in to their crazy plan! I twisted the ring on my finger and brought it up to try to catch his eye. The firelight glinted off the initials AF. I forced my will towards capturing Avdar's gaze, but my will hit an invisible wall. I pushed against it and heard Dani gasp next to me as she realized what I was trying to do. Still pushing, I felt that wall give, just slightly and saw a look of surprise cross Avdar's face.

"Devon, stop!" Dani whispered, urgently pulling on my arm. The heat in the room intensified, but only my father, Dani, and I were sweating. The fire seemed to make Avdar stronger and I could see him reaching for more strength. I quickly switched my intent and started to draw power away from the fire, away from Avdar. The flames flickered until it died down, flickering lightly at the logs.

Surprise turned into pleasure at my show of strength and Avdar tore his eyes away from my gaze. "Julian, he is strong. I am pleased." My father smiled weakly and turned a glare towards me.

I glared back, shook Dani's grip from my arm, and glanced around. All of the Daïmonids had moved further into the room and had circled around Avdar and me, trapping me within their circle. Needing to escape, I threw an arm out, and my whirlwind flew towards the Daïmonids between me and the door. It lifted two of them into the air and pushed them into the wall, where they remained pinned.

I looked at my father and Dani, then shook my head and hurried towards the door without saying another word. I needed to come up with a plan. I was not giving up my soul, or my body. I needed to talk to Avery.

Chapter 22

Cole

As the car pulled into a parking spot in front of the tea shop, I had to hold myself back from reaching for Avery's hand. We had driven from the dance to her place in almost complete silence. Even though I shouldn't care, I kept thinking about the moment I realized Avery wasn't dancing with our group. I had spotted Devon earlier, and immediately looked over in his direction. Sure enough, Avery was dancing with him. My reaction was instinctive, and intense! I wanted her to have a great night, but with me, not him. I could feel myself tense up again and realized that I had unknowingly reached out for her hand and was holding it hard. She was trying to pull it away.

"Sorry," I said, letting her hand go. I noticed she quietly stretched out her fingers and twisted her ring on her finger.

Wincing, I reached out my hand and brushed my thumb over the top of her hand. I said sorry again, and then drew my hand back.

"It's okay," she said quietly. "I keep thinking about what's going to happen tomorrow."

"Yeah, tomorrow." Uncomfortable, I changed the subject. "I had a lot of fun tonight. Well, with the exception of that one dance you had with Devon." I frowned when I saw her smile slightly. Ignoring it, I shifted in my seat so that I was facing Avery. I took a look in the rearview mirror, and glanced around us quickly, making sure we were alone.

"I had fun tonight," she said, smiling slightly. The light over the door of the store cast a shadow over half of her face, but the other half was very well lit.

"I think it's silly that you are thinking of keeping watch from your car. Maybe it would be okay if you slept on the couch?" Avery glanced over her shoulder towards the shop. I could see a light under the door that led back to the apartment. "It looks like my aunt is up, I could ask her if you want?"

"I think it's better if I stay out here and make sure you don't have any surprise visitors," I stated calmly, knowing that I wouldn't be anywhere close to Avery tomorrow night.

"Okay," she replied and started to turn towards the door to get out. Surprised, I reached for her arm.

"Wait a minute, I have something for you." I had argued with myself about giving her anything, but I had bought her this gift before my orders had changed and I really wanted to give it to her, even with everything that was going to go down. I reached over her to pull a small, gold gift-wrapped box out of the glove compartment. I held it out to her and surprised, she gently took it out of my hand. "Happy Birthday," I said softly, letting go of her hand so she could open the present.

"You didn't want to wait until we were all together tomorrow?" She looked up and I shook my head.

"I wanted to give this to you tonight, when we were by ourselves." I nudged the package toward her and said, "Open it. It's nothing big. I just saw it in a store window a couple of weeks ago and it reminded me of you."

She pulled at the bow and loosened the paper so a small white box was revealed. She pulled the lid off and revealed a delicate gold necklace with a smoothly polished amethyst crystal pendant shaped like an arrowhead. "It's beautiful," she said, looking at me curiously. She reached out a finger to touch it. "Will you put it on me?"

She pulled out the necklace and gave it to me, then turned her back to me and lifted her hair off her neck. I cursed quietly to myself and struggled to attach the clasp. When it connected I shifted back towards the window behind me, needing to put some space between us, my emotions conflicted.

She pulled the visor down, illuminating a mirror, and examined the necklace. She turned to me with a smile on her face.

At that look, I started to speak quickly, feeling like I was sinking in quicksand. "I read somewhere that it's believed that amethysts help seers open their minds, gives them focus and some sort of protection. And well, I thought you'd like it."

When I was getting ready for the dance tonight, I saw the gift sitting on my dresser and grabbed it. I had bought it when I was really falling for Avery. Oh hell, who was I kidding, I had fallen for her. I ran a hand through my hair and focused on her.

"I think it's beautiful," she said, and she reached up to give me a kiss on the cheek in thanks. Just when her lips started to touch my skin, I moved my head so that I was kissing her lips. I just wanted this one perfect moment, it was too irresistible to pass up. I pressed a little harder and what started as a soft kiss of thanks became something a little more desperate. All of my anxiety and mixed emotions poured from me into her and as I lifted my head I gazed into her hazel eyes that were now a bright green and felt regret and pain. I kissed her gently on the forehead and looked away quickly, missing the look of confusion and disappointment on her face.

I had a knot in my stomach as I said, "You should go inside. I'll see you tomorrow." I faced forward, creating some distance between the two of us, and reached out to turn on the car.

I heard a confused, "Okay," and felt a cool brush of air as she opened the car door.

"Thanks for the fun night. And the gift." Avery said and I responded with a quiet good night. I had a lot to think about and prepare myself for.

Chapter 23

Avery

The store didn't open until 10 a.m., so when I heard a knock on the door at 8:30, I glanced down at my pink tank and pajama shorts covered in kittens and gave a mental shrug.

When I saw it was Devon, I cursed. I ran my fingers through my hair and opened the door, peeking out around the edge at him. I should've probably been nervous about meeting him alone, after last night, but at his smile, my nervousness fled.

"Hey." I saw him glance down at my pajamas, his lips twisting into a smile. "Nice pj's. You like cats, huh?" I shrugged, tugging my shorts down slightly as I opened the door wide, letting him follow me into the house.

As we passed a chair, I grabbed a sweatshirt off the back and slipped it on. "Did you eat some breakfast? I was just making tea and we have some blueberry-citrus muffins that Brenna made yesterday." The kettle whistled, and at his nod, I got down another cup and some loose tea. I put the tea, cups, and muffins onto a tray and carried them to the back patio. It was a beautiful California fall morning, warm and crystal clear.

"I wanted to talk to you about what happened at the dance last night." Devon looked at me anxiously, his blue eyes having turned dark in concern.

"Cole said you tried to mesmerize me?" Instead of accusing him it came out as more of a question. I peeked up at him as I sipped my tea, confused at my feelings I reached up and felt the amethyst pendant hidden under my sweatshirt and put my hand down when I thought how weird Cole acted after he gave it to me, kissing me and then pushing me away. I refocused on Devon when he leaped up out of his chair.

"No!" Devon paced a length in front of the table. He looked around at the backyard and sat back down again. As he sat, I noticed a few blackbirds fly into the backyard and land in the jacaranda tree behind him. Some purple petals fluttered down to the ground.

"That was an accident! I am a Mesmer, I mean, I inherited that talent from my grandmother, but last night was so strange! I mean, in order to Mesmerize anyone, you have to have intent. And I didn't! Plus, I would never do that to you!" He spoke urgently into my eyes.

I thought about it and realized that I had never felt threatened by Devon. I nodded. "I believe you," I said. "You have had so many other opportunities and never had before. What do you think happened?" I was honestly curious. Ever since last week's assignment, Devon and I had been starting to act like we were friends.

"Maybe it was our rings reacting to each other in a new way, but honestly I don't know." He looked down at his hands and fiddled with his ring. "You're not mad?" He asked curiously.

"No. Of course not. I mean, once I got home and thought about it, I remembered how upset you were.

Although, Cole seemed pretty upset," I said, frowning slightly when I thought of Cole.

"Yeah. Well, he doesn't know me as well as you do." He looked at me hopefully and sat up straighter when I smiled at him.

I reached for a muffin and took a piece off the top and put it in my mouth and nodded my agreement. "True."

"There was another reason why I wanted to talk to you this morning," he said quietly, and at my nod, continued. "I found out a little more about our rings the other night, and, well, there's a situation."

"A situation?" I put the muffin back down on the plate and anxiously started to pick at the bottom of my sleeve. *What else could go wrong?* I thought.

"Yes, as you know, I'm also part Elemental, and well, my father has hooked up with some bad guys who are going to um, try to steal your powers, then inhabit my body and steal my soul." He rushed through that sentence as if trying to get rid of it. I looked at him in shock.

"Wait, inhabit your body? Like possession?" I'm not sure why I focused on that instead of the stealing my powers part of his sentence. Devon nodded.

As he explained his father and Avdar's plans, the beautiful morning started to turn chilly and I shivered at the abrupt change. I noticed the Jacaranda tree behind Cole was now filled with crows and the blackbirds had flown away. One of the crows dropped to the ground behind Devon and turned into a Daïmonid.

I stood up abruptly and squeaked out a warning, my chair scraping loudly against the concrete. Devon spun around to see what shocked me. When he saw the Daïmonid, his face twisted in anger.

"What do you think you're doing here? Spying on me?" Devon flung a hand out and the Daïmonid was pushed back by a force of wind and hit the tree trunk, impaling himself on a low hanging branch. With a pop he disappeared.

Another Daïmonid dropped out of the tree and started forward. I put up a shield so that he slammed quickly to a halt. "What are they doing here?" Frantically, I looked at Devon, as all of a sudden three more dropped out of the tree. I moved to his side.

"Insurance, I guess. If Avdar is supposed to get my body, they need to make sure that I've accepted their plan. I didn't leave the meeting last night in a very accepting mood." I could see Devon looking around the backyard, and then smile.

"You've got a sprinkler system! Awesome, this should be quick." He reached out a hand for me to grasp, and I felt power draw from him to me. Suddenly a vision entered my mind of a spray of water disintegrating a Daïmonid and I gestured to the side of the yard. A garden hose rose up on the other side of the lawn, and I sent a thought to the nozzle, which suddenly sprayed water all over the backs of the Daïmonids, making them scream and pop. Devon dropped my hand and the hose dropped to the ground.

"Did you feel that?" I squealed, reaching out my hand to him. Devon took a quick step away, and I shook my head calming down a bit. "We shared a thought too, well, at least I think that's what we were doing?" I looked at him and he nodded, his hands shoved into the front pocket of his jeans. "You don't need to be afraid of me, I won't do it again!" I was amazed, and truthfully empowered by what had just happened.

"It's not that, but that adds another level of danger to this situation," he said to me and I nodded, seeing his point. He looked back over his shoulder to where the

Daïmonid first landed on my lawn, and then back at me with a determined look on his face. "They don't just want to kill you, they want me to steal your powers so that I have this huge amount of power, and then somehow, they think I am going to give my body to Avdar to inhabit." He looked at me grimly. "And we just found out that you and I can share power. With what just happened, I'm sure they've figured out I've told you their plans."

I looked at Devon in sympathy. What kind of father would ask his son to sacrifice himself like this? *Of course, my own isn't father of the year*, I thought grimly. *It's just another thing we have in common.* I held out my hand to him, and when he took it, I pulled him into a hug. "I'm sorry Devon, this is just horrible."

With my head on his chest, I could hear his heartbeat speed up. I felt a tug on my hair and I looked up at him, surprised at what I saw. Devon was smiling happily down at me.

"Don't worry about it, I have had many years to get used to this disappointment from my father. But I appreciate that you're concerned." He gave me a kiss on the forehead and tugged me in for another hug.

"We have the whole day to figure out a plan, right?" I was convinced that with this new power we had a chance.

"Sure, let me call everyone. We were supposed to get together today for my birthday anyway. We'll just make it a birthday war meeting!" He smiled grimly and let me go. I went inside to get the phone to make some calls.

Chapter 24

Cole

I was immediately irritated when I knocked on the door and Devon opened it. I could hear the sound of Summer and Avery talking behind him. As I stepped forward to push my way past him, he stepped into me pushing me back outside, closing the door behind him.

"I think you and I need to have a little talk before we go back inside." Devon looked at me grimly and walked towards my car. He turned around and leaned against the hood.

Expecting something like this I ran a hand through my hair and nodded. "Okay, talk." I shoved my hands into my jeans pocket and looked him over. Devon didn't look like he'd gotten much sleep last night, dark circles shadowed his eyes, and his expression was intense. I know I had that same grim look in my eyes, but for a different reason. I straightened my shoulders and faced him.

"You're her Guardian?" He nodded towards the house, looking angry.

I gave him a slow nod, and he pushed off the car and stalked towards me. "You know more than what you've been telling her then." I clenched my hands at my side and started gathering energy.

I nodded again. "I know that your family is mixed up with one of the factions that is against Avery keeping her powers tonight. I know that your father has had meetings with the Daïmonids, and I know that my father is mixed up in this somehow," I said.

"Check. Check. And Check." Devon stopped in front of me, his face an inch from mine and looked me directly in the eyes looking angry. "So which side do you land on?"

"What side do you think?" I released the energy I was holding and pushed his shoulder, making him take a large step back, and I took a step away from him. Shit. I didn't need this guy coming at me, making things more difficult. "I'm going to be outside her house, in my car tonight, watching, just to make sure she's safe when she starts her transition." At least that was the plan I had told Avery.

"Outside her house isn't going to help. My family has figured out how to get into her transition dream with her, and they plan on stealing her powers right after she gets them." Well, crap, that changes everything! If his family is going to be in her transition, that means my duty to kill her has been sped up to today! My mind replayed the scene in the car last night, when I gave her the present. Our kiss. I locked those emotions down.

Devon swung an arm out, and I noticed that the tree across the street was filled with crows. "They have Daïmonids watching our every move today." He lifted his head and looked at the Jacaranda tree next to the front door.

I nodded, and said softly, "The Sentinel also has the Elementals keeping an eye on us." I motioned to the blackbirds lining that tree. A soft rustling filled the air and a bird flew down out of the tree and landed in front of us. The bird fluttered its wings and then started to shimmer, until the Sentinel stood in front of the two of us. I immediately straightened my back, standing at attention.

At the sound of wings behind us, I glanced towards the crows, and saw one fly out of the tree and land across the street.

"Shit. Avdar." I heard Devon mutter under his breath. I turned back to Avery's father.

"Sir." I nodded at him, but saw that he was ignoring me, looking at Devon.

"Julian's son, right?" The Sentinel looked at Devon briefly and then Avdar across the street. He turned his back to them, as if he wasn't threatened by their presence.

"Cole." As he started to speak, the front door opened and Avery stood there. She looked surprised when she saw the Sentinel standing in front of her, but that surprise quickly turned to pleasure.

"Dad!" She rushed forward as if to throw her arms around her father, but he took a step back, grabbing her hands instead.

I glanced quickly over my shoulder at Devon, then made sure Avdar had not moved from across the street. My hands clenched into fists at my side, and I started to gather power.

"Avery, you need to go back inside." I said quickly, glancing at the Sentinel to see that he hadn't dropped her hands, but had held them out, as if taking a look at her. This was the first time he'd seen his daughter in person, and he was looking at her without any emotion on his face.

"Avery. Wow, you look so much like your mother. Beautiful. Happy Birthday." He leaned forward and gave her a small kiss on her check. At his words, Avery looked at Devon and me. I stared stoically back at her knowing she must be stunned by her father's rejection, but not able to act. Devon pulled her toward him and whispered something in her ear that made her relax back against him.

"Dad," she said, noticeably startled when Devon threw up a wall between them. Shocked, I glanced at the Sentinel to see his reaction, but he just stared at his daughter with a slight frown on his face.

"Avery. Go back inside, this is too dangerous right now!" Devon glanced towards Avdar, who had started to walk across the street toward us. Crows dropped out of the tree and landed on the ground as Daïmonids, flanked his position. In response, more blackbirds flew out of the jacaranda tree, and changed into Elementals. They lined up next to my car to face them.

Devon pushed past the Sentinel and me trying to hurry Avery through the door. Conflicted between my duty to the Sentinel and my feelings for Avery, I let him. Devon almost had her there but she shrugged away from him, back toward her father. She held out her hands in front of her, as if to grasp her father's again, but stopped in surprise. Staring at her hands, I was surprised to see the Daïmonid and Elemental energy siphon toward her in strands of red, gold, and green. In her confusion, it seemed that she was collecting power. Shocked, I watched as that power disappeared inside her, her hair blowing out behind her and her clothes clinging tightly to her body as the power whipped around her.

The door behind her banged open and Summer and Brenna stepped out, quickly taking in the scene. Summer stepped forward to the empty space on Avery's right. Devon, who was already on her left, reached out and joined hands with her.

As they did, that power she had been siphoning flashed, and with a loud pop, everyone went still, except myself, her father, Devon, and Avdar.

When I saw Avery and Devon's joined hands, and realized that action joined their power together, my own hands clenched at my sides in preparation for something. Unsure, I looked up into Avery's eyes and saw them flicker to mine also with uncertainty, but she kept holding Devon's hand. Devon stepped forward so that he was blocking her from her father.

"Sir." Devon's eyes blazed an arctic blue, and his silhouette started to shimmer. "I don't think you just dropped in to wish your daughter a happy birthday. Considering she's been here a month, and you haven't even tried to see her."

Avery nodded slowly, and glanced from me to Devon, "You don't think he's here to help?" I shook my head just slightly, and saw Devon do the same. My thoughts were torn, I knew my duty, but didn't want her blindsided by her father's ambivalence.

"Now son, I am only here to wish her well on her journey tonight." I saw her father gaze thoughtfully at his daughter and take a step forward. Then he seemed to change his mind and looked over at Brenna instead. He flicked a finger and she jerked forward a step. They exchanged a long look, then her father turned abruptly and he and his men disappeared in a flurry of wings. Blackbirds dived and flew off over the trees.

At their movement, the spell was broken and Avdar spoke up from the middle of the street. "I'm so sorry I interrupted such a," and he paused, smiling grimly, "happy family reunion." He chuckled softly. "We'll see you soon, Avery. Devon." After a glance at me, he and the Daïmonids disappeared with a pop.

Avery glanced around at the rest of us and said, her voice wavering with tears, "Is anyone going to fill me in on what that was all about?" She looked over at her aunt, whose eyes were also bright with tears.

Brenna nodded slightly. "I think it's time I told you the truth, or at least what your mother wrote to me." She disappeared through the door, and with a glance at Avery, Summer followed her inside. Avery, who was still holding Devon's hand, looked at me questioningly. I had no idea what to say to her and I hated to disappoint her. I know we are friends and if we, or she were normal we could've been so much more. Even with those feelings swirling inside of me, how do you tell someone your own father wants you dead? And he wants me to be the one to kill you?

I took a deep breath and let it out slowly. Looking again at their joined hands I saw the threat their joined power would represent. I felt a burning in my chest and my resolve solidified. I had trained my whole life to protect my people, and I was not going to let my family, or them down.

Chapter 25

Avery

Ben and Ana had shown up as Cole started talking, so we all moved into my backyard and sat around the table on the patio. Cole was seated across the table, with Ben on his right. Ana, and Summer were seated on either side of me, and Devon stood at my back occasionally pacing the small stone deck.

"So, the plan our fathers set in motion almost five years ago, setting me up as your Guardian, your father's rise through the ranks to Sentinel of our race, was so that if you were the prophesied one, you would have a Guardian." Cole pointed at himself and I nodded. As he took a breath to continue, I noticed his purple eyes had turned a darker shade, so that they were almost black. He ran a hand through his hair, but then changed the motion of his arm and tugged lightly on his eyebrow piercing.

"What Devon said out there was true. Why hasn't my father come to see me in the month and a half that I've lived in Dover?" As I asked the question, Brenna came out of the house to join in our conversation.

"That's partly my fault." Brenna said, moving forward to lay a hand on my shoulder. "I don't trust him. In the letter that your mother left me, she said that at first she and your father communicated frequently, but over the past two years she hadn't heard from him at all." She looked up from pouring the tea into a glass and met my eyes. "After she lost contact, she felt like you both were being watched. She'd had an incident with an Elemental while you were in Texas, and if she hadn't had that ring on," and she nodded down at my hand that was twisting the ring around my finger, "she would've died then. The ring shielded her from his attack and reflected his power back at him, killing him."

"That would be why we had picked up and moved so quickly." I said quietly, and Brenna nodded her agreement. I remembered when we were in Texas and my mother must have still hoped that my father would join us. It seemed like she was always looking for him wherever we went. Now that I thought about it, after we left Texas, after her attack, my mom stopped mentioning my father.

Cole spoke up, saying "Why would they have set me up as her Guardian if they were going to harm her?"

Brenna shrugged. "That confused me as well but taking advantage of the training you were giving her was only going to help, so I didn't want to stand in your way."

Devon finally spoke up from behind me, "And it's a good thing she's had some sort of training with all of the Daïmonid activity."

"Exactly." Cole looked relieved, even if that support was coming from Devon.

"But you still don't trust him?" I looked at my aunt hoping for a different answer but was disappointed to see her shaking her head.

"Today's actions just confirmed it for me. I'm sorry, honey, but he wasn't acting like a father. He was acting like a Sentinel."

I had a few memories of my father and the man I saw earlier, although he looked like him, didn't act like the man in my memories. My father had been full of laughter, hugs and love. I flashed back to that photo of my dad throwing me into the air, laughing. The man I met earlier was a stranger. "I think the fact that he hasn't even contacted me since I've been here say's it all."

"That's not strictly true, honey. I've communicated with your father a couple of times. He always arrives as a blackbird, and I have seen him lingering in the backyard occasionally." My aunt nodded toward a tree in the backyard that even now had several blackbirds in it, watching and listening to us.

"Through them, he has been keeping an eye on you. But he can't be seen talking to you. Not until after you gain your powers and the Elementals see that you aren't the girl from the prophecy," Cole said slowly and softly, glancing over at the birds.

"Sugar, that does make sense. I mean, blackbirds are common for the area, but I've noticed a lot of them lately. At school, and here, but not necessarily everywhere. They aren't at my home, Ana, are they at yours?"

Ana shook her head quickly, her freckles whirling until her skin took on the slightly grey shade of the stone wall behind her. "I've heard some of the kids at school commenting about a blackbird infestation as well, so it is unusual."

"Okay, so he's watching me. But when the Daïmonids have attacked, he hasn't interfered at all," I said in a rush.

"He can't." Cole spoke up quickly. "He is evaluating you to see if you are the prophesied one. After tonight, I'm sure, he'll come forward. Once he knows for sure." As he said this, the blackbirds took off and flew out of the backyard. He let out a huge breath and I looked at him in question.

"I just feel better when they're gone," he said, and Ben nodded as well.

"Bruh, now that I know who they are, it's like spies are everywhere." He reached an arm over Summer's shoulder next to him and whispered in her ear. She sent an elbow into his gut and blushed. Ana hid a small smile and quirked an eyebrow at me.

I laughed, "I'm sure my father isn't watching the two of you make out anywhere, Ben." Everyone at the table laughed, glad for the release in tension. I noticed, though, that Cole and Devon didn't laugh, staring intently at each other.

"We do have some other news we need to fill you all in on." I looked over my shoulder at Devon and smiled slightly telling him it was his turn. Devon, looking serious, took the seat my aunt vacated. He watched Brenna walk into the house and turned to the table.

"This is what's going on with my family." He proceeded to fill everyone in about his father's plans for him, and the fact that he was supposed to steal my powers before getting possessed by Avdar.

"Dude, that's vicious." Ben looked at Devon with sympathy, and Summer chimed in her support. Ana just turned a slightly green tint.

I looked at Cole, to see his reaction, and noticed a slightly glazed look in his eyes.

"Cole?" I called softly. He looked at me and cleared his throat.

"So Devon and I were talking earlier, and because his sister and he will be in your transition, then it's not going to do any good if I'm sitting outside your house, is it?" I shook my head.

"I'll need to get into your dream as well." As he spoke, a cloud covered the sun, and the backyard darkened. The cloud moved on quickly, and as the others chimed in their support, the glare from the sun made me squint towards Devon, whose back was to it.

"So how is everyone entering my transition?" I asked the question everyone was thinking.

"I haven't really talked to Dani since last night, so I don't have a clue how we are supposed to do it," Devon stated and looked down at his hands.

"I think I can help you all with that." Brenna spoke from the back door and brought an old book out and set it on the table. It was bound in leather and had a large eye imprinted on the cover. "Even though my power was in the knowledge of herbs, I do have the family book of charms." She opened it up and started flipping through the pages. Dust filled the air, and a light musty smell lingered, making Summer sneeze delicately. Devon raised a hand and a soft breezed dispelled the scent.

"I know there's a spell in here somewhere. I remember reading about this charm when I was younger and experimenting a bit." She flipped another couple of pages and then stood up straight. "Here it is." She pointed down at the page and we all leaned forward to read the words at the top: Dream Traveler's Charm.

"A Dream Traveler's Charm?" I loved the idea of a charm that would help bring everyone into my transition. I looked at the spell trying to read the ingredients upside down.

My aunt skimmed a finger down the list of ingredients and straightened up from the table. "I have most of these, but there are a couple of things I'm going to need to go out and get."

"I hope it will work?" I meant to say it like a statement but Brenna took it as a question and I noticed everyone else also looking at Brenna for the answer.

"This is your Great Aunt Ailene's book of charms. She was one of the most famous Spell Seekers in our family. Her gift was for charm making and spell casting. If anything is going to help us get into your transition, it's a spell from Ailene's book." She smiled and said this with such confidence that we all sat back in relief. "So, I'll go out and get the rest of these ingredients. I'm going to need to spend the rest of the day making all of these charms for everyone." She looked around the table at us, and then smiled. "Didn't you all have something planned for Avery's birthday today?"

Summer and Ana chimed in about fun things to do and everyone started talking about our plans for the day. I looked at Brenna and asked, "Are you going to need some help putting these together?"

"No. This is my part to play, so you all go on and have a nice day. All of you are going to need to be in the right frame of mind to do this tonight." I gave her a smile of relief and thanks and she put her arm around me for a quick hug.

"Happy Birthday eve, Avery." She said softly and picked up the book and walked quickly back into the house and shut the door.

"What did you want to do today Avery?" Ana asked quietly, and the rest of the group hushed. I looked over at Devon, then around the table.

"I want to learn how to surf!"

Devon grinned, pleased that I wanted to learn something that he enjoyed. The others rose to their feet, and we made plans to meet down at the beach in an hour. Devon remained behind with me, but Cole, after glancing suspiciously at him, said he'd be back in a half hour to make the drive with us, and left to pick up his board shorts.

Chapter 26

Devon

When we got to the beach, Cole, Avery and I started hauling our stuff down to where Summer, Ben, and Ana were set up under Summer's huge hot pink umbrella. I hauled the big bag full of food that Avery had packed up for us, and set it down next to Summer's head, spraying her with a little sand.

"Hey!" She sat up and swiped at her cheek.

"Sorry." I said, glancing over at Avery as she pulled a large striped beach towel out of her bag and anchored the corners with two of her flip flops. She set up her lotions next to her. Cole set his cooler next to Avery and pulled off his t-shirt. Avery handed him some sunscreen.

"Who's going to surf?" I asked glancing around at the group. Ben raised a hand, as did Avery and Cole. Summer shivered in disgust, and Ana hesitantly nodded.

"Sugar, it may surprise you, but I don't like water." Summer said with a shudder and Avery laughed lightly.

"What, can't get your fur wet?" She threw a Diet Coke to Summer, who caught it without looking in her direction. She popped the top.

"Exactly." She said bluntly and took a large gulp of the soda. "Thanks for the drink!"

Ben, Cole, and I rented the boards at a shack down the beach, and after applying sunscreen liberally, the five of us headed towards the water.

"Okay, who hasn't surfed before?" I asked the group. Avery raised her hand and looked around at the others.

"Seriously?" She said when she saw she was the only one with their hand raised. "Well, I've been a bit busy!" She looked over at me and asked, "Who's going to give me the basics?"

Cole stepped forward at the same time I did. I stopped and looked between him and Avery. Avery hesitated, looking at Cole apologetically, and took a step towards me. Ben sensing the awkwardness grabbed Cole and tugged him towards the water, giving Cole a push that had him tumbling into the water, laughing.

"I thought I was going to have to fight him for you," I teased her, pleased that she had picked me. I reached for her board to carry it towards the water.

"Oh stop." She chided. "He's just being protective."

"Yeah, Okay." I set her board point down in the sand, the incoming waves gently lapping at it. I took her hand and tugged her towards the water with just the one board.

"We aren't taking mine?" she asked as she looked back at her board and followed me into the water.

"Nope. First, we are going to get on the board and practice balancing. Hop on." She climbed onto the board and scooted up towards the front her legs slightly parted. I climbed on the back between her legs, my chest just over her calves. I glanced down at her bikini-clad butt and then up again quickly. I tried to hide a grin as I kicked my legs. She started paddling us out to the other surfers. As we approached, a wave broke over us, and we pushed through to calmer water. Avery sat up on the board, shaking her wet hair out of her eyes and I sat behind her watching the other surfers for a moment.

Ben was a natural. He moved through the water so fast, and when I looked closely, I saw faint webbing between his fingers. He caught a wave, stood up, and surfed down the line of the wave, cutting right and left. His back foot cut the board into the water, making a line of water jet out behind him. All of a sudden he sprung into the air and did a flip, his feet never losing contact with his board. I looked at Avery in amazement and she grinned.

"I'm not surprised he's great at this!" She said with a laugh, wiggling her fingers at me. "He's part frog, you know, suction toes." From the beach I could hear a loud whoop and Summer's voice screaming with laughter, rooting him on. Ben rode that wave all the way down to the beach, getting out of the water and shaking himself so water sprayed all over Summer. Avery laughed, watching them.

I saw Cole glance over at us, "I'm going to take this one," he said looking at the incoming wave, and I nodded back. Cole made eye contact with Avery one more time, and then flipped his hair out of his eyes and moved his board out so he could catch the oncoming wave. As he stood up on the board, I could see one hand balled into a fist down at his side, while the other was held out wide to help him balance. He flung his fist out and what was a pretty small wave grew quickly, turning into a huge, storm enraged wave. As the lip curled, Cole used his back foot to cut the board into the water and shoot through the curl, his right hand trailing upon the water in the wave beside him. As he came through the curl at the end of the wave, a spray of water shot out with a large burst almost spitting him forward, so that he approached the beach at a very fast speed. He waved an arm and the sand moved forward to gently stop his movement, and he rode the board up the beach and stopped next to Summer and Ben, who were cheering. When the board stopped he stepped lightly off onto the sand with a small bow. He looked back at us and gave a brief wave.

I looked over at Ana, who was sitting calmly on her board. I nodded her forward and she smiled at Avery. "Looks like I'm up!" She scooted down on her board and started paddling quickly towards the next wave. This wave was a much more reasonable size than the power enhanced wave that Cole rode. Ana very efficiently got up on the board and crouched down to balance. I could see her board move back and forth on the water, but only Ana's bathing suit was visible. I looked down at Avery, and she giggled.

"Chameleon." I guessed, and she nodded. "You've got some interesting friends!" She laughed and nodded again.

"Including you." At her words, a feeling of warmth went through me and I grabbed her hand to tug her back towards me kissing the back of her hand. I looked into her eyes, which had turned a bright green, "Thanks, milady." I gave her a cocky grin.

"Are you ready to give it a try?" I asked, gesturing at the next wave. She bit her bottom lip and gave a nod and started paddling. As we crested the wave, I helped her to stand and took my place behind her. She wobbled slightly, but I held her waist lightly, stabilizing her. I showed her how to position a leg back for balance and we rode the wave in until we hit the beach. I calmed the water, making sure it was a smooth ride. She tumbled off the board, laughing in triumph and I grinned back at her. Summer and Ana came rushing down to give her a hug, and Ana grabbed her hand to tug her back into the water. I gave her my board and walked back up to our beach towels and sat down next to Cole. He looked at me a moment and then smirked.

"Nice moves," he said. I looked back at the water, watching Ana and Ben tutor Avery on the next wave. Yes, and if we all survived this, I'd step up my game.

I was back out in the water with Avery, Ben, and Cole. Summer and Ana were sunning on the beach. Avery was on her own board, and was sitting up watching the waves come in. Ben moved up to take the next one but stopped and gasped, pulling his feet out of the water. I saw Cole sit up abruptly and look at the water around us. The temperature of the water had not changed, but the water started to boil. Avery, who had been lounging on her board, sat up straight and eyed Cole. I looked over at Cole to see he had his hands curled into fists, drawing on his power. I moved my board over closer to Avery's and gathered my own power.

"Cole, what's going on?" Avery called over to him, but he didn't answer. He kept scanning the water around us. Avery's hair was shifting wildly as she drew her own power.

All of a sudden, I felt a brush against my foot and I was yanked off my board. I heard Avery cry out, then my head was under the water. I reached down to my foot and opened my eyes when I felt something gripping it. Trying to uncurl the tentacle from around my ankle, I gazed down into the bright milky white eye of a Merdaïmon.

Shocked, I struggled to remove its tentacle. Merdaïmons did not usually come this close to the surface of the water, preferring the depths of the sea. They were man shaped, except in the place of arms they had tentacles with large octopus like suckers that could rip into flesh. Their single, milky white eye was sightless, but they used their other senses to capture prey. The Merdaïmon's mouth was a dark tooth-filled circle in his face. It was pursed into a kiss, sucking water and my life force into its body. Thanking my father for those tutors who worked with me on using my water and fire gifts at the same time, I sent a jet of air to create pockets around my hands. Using my power over fire, I drew heat from the sun glimmering through the water to fire up my hands. I gripped them around both tentacles and shot flames into its body, making it dissolve into the water.

I swam for the surface to gulp in air. I glanced around and saw boiling water everywhere, and Cole, Ben, and Avery were nowhere to be found. I gathered more power from the air and sun and dove back in to find Avery. I saw her struggling against another Merdaïmon, its mouth gaping open. I could see her life force, a bright green color, start to drain towards its mouth. She went still, and I saw the Merdaïmon stop and quickly release her, disappearing into the waters depths. Seeing her out of danger, I used my power over air to encapsulate her head in a large air bubble. I could see her gasp in a breath. When she caught her breath, I looked at her questioningly, and saw her mouth what looked like "I talked to it." *Huh*, I thought, *a new talent*. Not Elemental, though. I'd have to remember to ask her about it later. I looked down at her leg seeing that the Merdaïmons tentacles had cut her leg slightly, and blood trickled into the water.

The Merdaïmons seemed to be avoiding us. Avery and I turned in a slow circle, trying to see how Ben and Cole were faring. Three Merdaïmons were swimming rapidly towards us, their tentacles pushing the water behind them to impel their bodies forward.

I caught sight of Ben struggling to our right. I motioned towards him, and Avery and I, our heads still encapsulated in the air bubbles, swam towards him to help him escape. All of a sudden, the two Merdaïmons who had him entrapped in their tentacles exploded with loud pops. Ben, twice his normal size, his skin lime green in color, looked towards us, his eyes half lidded. He leaped through the water and struck at one of the Merdaïmons who had followed us over to him. Avery and I joined hands, our legs moving, keeping us stationary in the water. This time, instead of draining my own power into her, I drew power from the sun and water and fed both of us. Avery, eyes widening in surprise, nodded and closed them. The warmth from our power spread outward until the two of us glowed a bright electric blue and we lit up the water around us for a hundred yards. Ben had moved in Cole's direction, but at the light behind him, turned around to take a look at what was happening. Avery, using our combined power, started to push the water around us, forming a small whirlpool. Helping her, I pushed more power to her which she used to focus her own power. Her eyes closed, I saw her lips moving. The water began to whirl, gathering Merdaïmons, until they were swirling around us. Only the water directly around us stayed still. Ben, seeing that we didn't need his help, swam in Cole's direction.

Using the power I had gathered from the air, I created a waterspout, directing our whirlpool up out of the ocean into the air. The Merdaïmons seemed to be no longer struggling, and I snuck a glance at Avery. Her eyes were now open and she stared at the Merdaïmons in concentration. As the water swirled upward, the Merdaïmons were drawn over our heads. The waterspout grew to five hundred feet in the air, and nodding at Avery, we released our power, leaving the Merdaïmons hanging with no water to support them. Unable to survive in just air, their bodies turned white and dispersed with a burst of bubbles, like a small fireworks display.

Having beaten our opponents, Avery and I looked towards Cole and Ben. Cole, air bubble surrounding his head and blood streaming from his right leg, had been drawing on his Earth power to fling sharp objects from the floor of the ocean to pepper the Merdaïmons, distracting them from being able to steal his life force. He had five surrounding him. As Cole distracted them, Ben would swim behind them and pull them into a death frog hold, poisoning them with his skin. As the last one disintegrated, Ben and Cole swam for the surface, Ben's body rapidly returning to his normal size. Avery and I followed, the air bubbles around our heads dispersing as our heads broke the surface.

Avery flung herself towards me and I reached out and scooped her close. She gave me a quick hug and then swam over to hug Cole. Ben opened his arms, and without hesitation, she also gave him a quick hug.

She opened her mouth to say something, but then shook her head and started swimming towards the beach. We were all breathing heavily, and one of us was injured pretty badly. Our boards on the other hand were gone. We swam towards shore, where Summer and Ana paced the beach.

Chapter 27

Cole

I limped up the shore looking back to see Devon and Avery just leaving the water. Ben was rummaging through the cooler Avery had brought, taking out all of the napkins.

"Dude, sit down and let me take a look at that leg." He found a cylinder of antiseptic spray in his bag and came over to me. I sat down on my towel and carefully examined my leg. The cut wasn't too bad. I grabbed a wad of napkins and held them up to the cut.

Avery ran up, flinging a spray of sand over everyone, flopping down on her knees next to me. "Are you okay?" She lifted the napkins up and took a look at the cut. At her small gasp, I glanced over at Devon. I heard a hiss, and a cold spray of antiseptic hit the cut, making me flinch.

"It's okay, it's just a small cut." I reached up and rubbed the end of my towel over my face and hair. I grabbed the bandage Ana was holding out to me with a nod of thanks. I noticed Devon sitting and applying some antiseptic to his own ankle. "You all right?" I asked, and he nodded.

Avery dabbed at some small cuts near her own ankle. "What were those things?" She asked as she looked over at me in horror.

"They are cousins to Daïmonids, but Merdaïmons can only be found in the ocean, though, and usually not this near the surface." I responded.

"It's a little weird that the Merdaïmons attacked like that isn't it?" Devon patted on the bandage Ana had given him and looked at me.

I nodded and looked away towards the ocean. I didn't want Devon to realize that I was the one who called in the Merdaïmons. I agonized on my way home to get my swim trunks about fulfilling my mission. I was torn between wanting to tell everyone to go to hell, and not wanting to disappoint my family. After what I'd learned earlier today though, I just wasn't sure that she wasn't going to hurt our people. Not on purpose, but her powers have grown tremendously, and now that she and Devon have joined their powers? The chance that she could get out of control was just too great.

The Sentinel had been waiting for me at my house when I arrived home earlier and it was his decision to call in the Merdaïmons. Unfortunately, they weren't given the message that only Avery was to be hurt. I lifted the napkins from my ankle and glanced over at Ben. I didn't want my other friends to be caught in the middle of all of this, but I couldn't warn them away without Avery finding out.

"Avery, what was it you said to me in the water?" Devon was asking and I turned to listen.

"Oh. I, well, it was really weird. It was like they were throwing pictures into my head, you know?" She was telling Devon, and I saw him nod.

"Like I did to you?" he said, and I sat up shocked.

"Yeah. Kind of, so I thought I'd try to project at them in return. I thought at them to play dead. I kind of pictured it?" She sounded proud, but confused, as she tried to explain what she'd done. "It seemed to work, because it just let go of me." She said and Devon grinned at her.

I was shocked at this information. They were talking like they had done something like this before? That wasn't an Elemental gift, though it sounded like some sort of an enhanced gift from her mother's side? *It just keeps getting worse*, I thought.

I looked at the group. Summer and Ben were sitting on a towel, holding hands, not paying any attention to their discussion. Ana was digging through the cooler handing out sodas, her freckles whirling madly in nervousness over what just happened, making her blend slightly into the sand. Devon and Avery shared a towel while talking quietly, but Devon glanced occasionally over to me. Catching my eye, he repeated his earlier statement.

"Cole, don't you think it's a huge coincidence that Merdaïmons, who have a very small population in the Pacific Ocean, would attack us for no reason?" I again nodded in agreement.

"I'm not positive that our conversations haven't been overheard. I'm thinking that someone tipped off the Merdaïmons to our being at the beach today." I looked over at Ben and shrugged. "It's a good thing Avery's getting her powers tonight; everything is escalating."

"Sugar, it was terrifying not being able to see what was happening to y'all." Summer's hand gripped Ben so tight, her knuckles turned white.

Ben flinched, "Ouch, tiger, lighten the grip!" Ben flexed his hand and waved it in the air like it burned. Summer hit him lightly on the shoulder and said, turning to Avery, "If someone's adding in Merdaïmons to the fight, who knows what's going to happen tonight. We should head back and see if Brenna's got those charms made up."

Everyone nodded their heads in agreement and started to gather their things.

Chapter 28

Avery

I watched Devon steer his car around another downed tree, the wind trying to wrestle control of the car away from him. He gripped the steering wheel so tightly his knuckles were white.

"What are the chances that the Santa Ana winds would start today?" I looked at Cole in the back seat, not wanting to distract Devon any more from driving. I heard another crack and I whipped my head around to look out the windshield. Another tree limb fell into the street and Devon cursed, slowing the car and steering around it.

"Santa Anas usually do hit this time of year, but I agree, the timing seems to be a bit coincidental." Devon looked at Cole in the back seat who was staring intently out the window.

"Cole." Cole glanced up and met his eyes in the rearview mirror. "Do you see something that we should be worried about?" Devon took a quick glance around and returned his eyes to Cole's.

"No, but anything could happen, so I'm just keeping an eye out." Cole answered grimly, and then returned to looking out the window, his eyes constantly scanning ahead.

I looked over at Devon to see him looking worriedly in the rearview. "What?" I whispered to him and reached over to touch his arm.

He just shook his head slightly and mouthed "later" to me. Should I be worried that something was going on that I didn't know about? Not like I've really got a handle on anything. Things had changed so quickly between Cole and me, and Devon, who used to kind of creep me out, was now my anchor. My life had done a 180 over the last couple of weeks. I looked at Devon out of the corner of my eye again and saw him relax as we turned onto my street. We pulled to the curb, with Ana, Summer, and Ben pulling up behind us. We braced against the wind and raced through the door of the store.

Brenna was in the front of the shop picking up some overturned chairs and a few items that had been blown off the shelves. She turned as we came through the door and exclaimed, "Thank goodness you all are back. This wind came up so suddenly, and it's so much worse than normal!" The wind rattled the windows behind us, and she shooed us through the door into our apartment.

"Does anyone want anything to drink?" I asked as I headed into the kitchen. I heard Summer and Ana fill my aunt in on what happened to us at the beach. When I came back into the room, she reached an arm out pulling me in for a hug. "Honey, I'm so glad you weren't hurt." I enjoyed the moment, her scent of black tea and vanilla embracing me with warmth. *I could get used to these hugs*, I thought, hugging my aunt back.

"Yeah, we got pretty lucky, Cole and Devon got the worst of the injuries. We are kind of worried over how everything is escalating so much." I said looking over at the counter where I noticed five black velvet bags. "You got the charms done?" I asked fingering one of the bags. She moved it away from me slightly.

"Don't touch these until right before you are all going into Avery's spiritual transition. Each bag will work for only one person, and you don't want to taint any with your own essence." Everyone had been eyeing the bags curiously, but at her words, backed up slightly, nervously putting their hands behind their backs.

Brenna laughed, "Don't worry, they should work fine tonight. I felt the earth hum when I finished each charm, so the potency will definitely work for each of you."

She looked around at everyone and the sand sticking to our skin. "Why don't you all take a break and go home to get cleaned up?"

I felt the salt on my skin and agreed with a nod. "Good idea. Why don't we meet back here at 11 p.m.?" Ana, Ben, and Summer stood to go, saying their goodbyes. I walked them to the door, Devon and Cole trailing behind me. Cole glanced between Devon and me and then gripped my arm lightly. As he did, the wind hit the windows with an extra loud shake, the door that I'd just latched swinging back and catching me in the shoulder. I stumbled back against Devon, breaking Cole's hold on my arm. Devon scooted me behind him and looked at Cole warily.

"See you back here later," Cole said evenly, looking at Devon, then glanced at me and quirked a smile. I smiled lightly back.

"Thanks for the fun at the beach." I said trying to make light of the attack.

"Yeah, fun." He said and gave a laugh. I watched him walk out to his car, the wind whipping his hair. The sunlight glinting off the windshield of his car made me squint as I watched him walk away.

Devon reached for my hand and I looked away from Cole driving off to look up into Devon's face. He had also been watching Cole's car with a small frown on his face. I tightened my grip on his hand and he looked down at me.

"What's wrong?" I asked him, pulling him away from the door as it shook again from the wind.

"There's something off about Cole. And what happened at the beach? I just don't like it. Are you sure he should be going with us tonight?" He looked down at me worriedly.

I hesitated, thinking over everything that had happened. Cole had been acting strange. I sighed, and then nodded. "Yes, if you all are going to be there, then he should, definitely. He's my Guardian. He'll be an extra set of hands and skills to make sure nothing goes wrong." I felt the ring on my hand growing warm and looked up at him.

"Yeah." He ran both of his hands up my arms until they cupped my shoulders. "It's just that there have been a lot of coincidences. Those winds sprung up kind of quickly, and Merdaïmons?" I shivered lightly as he kissed my forehead. "I don't have a good feeling about this," he said quietly, then walked out the door.

After Devon left, I joined my aunt in the kitchen where she was making a cup of tea. She gestured to her cup and I nodded. She reached up into the cabinet and grabbed another cup, pouring water into it. I packed my tea strainer full of some chamomile and let it steep. I sat down at our little dining room table and looked at my aunt who looked back at me with a raised eyebrow as she sipped her tea.

"I would love it if I didn't feel like I was going into this completely blind." I said to her, trying to hide my nervousness. I let the water drip out of the strainer and I laid it down on the saucer and lifted my cup. "If Mom were here, what do you think she'd want me to do?"

Brenna put down her cup and laid her hand on my own. "I know your mother would want you to be safe. Whatever you decide to do, it should be something that only you know. Don't share it with me, don't share it with Cole or your friends, and don't share it with Devon." She reached over to the window and threw it open. The sound of the breeze gently blowing through the leaves was surprising after the strong Santa Anas blowing earlier. I took a breath; the scent of lavender created a moment of peace. We sat there quietly, and then she looked at me again. "I have been waiting until your friends left to give you a couple of things." She got up and went over to a drawer in the kitchen and removed two items. My eyes looked first to the gift-wrapped package, but then I felt drawn to the other item. She laid a piece of black canvas on the counter.

"First, your gift," she said with a smile. She took the gift-wrapped package and presented it to me. I handled it gingerly, looking at the bright silver bow and pink paper. Presents were rare. My mom and I spent all of our money on essentials. We celebrated birthdays with a hug and a store-bought slice of cake.

I carefully unwrapped the present, savoring the moment, but Brenna gave me a pair of scissors and gestured for me to cut through the ribbon. I did and then tore into the wrapping paper. Inside was a cell phone. I looked at it, and then at her, knowing how much this cost. "Thank you!" I said jumping up and giving her a hug.

Brenna blushed and stammered a bit, looking pleased. "I want to be able to reach you in case of emergencies, and well, every teenager should have their own phone. Just don't go crazy! We don't have unlimited data or texting."

I laughed and promised not to overuse it. I took it out of the box and turned it on. It lit up immediately and I scrolled through the numbers. All of my friends' numbers were already in the phone.

I smiled, and Brenna laughed with me. "While you were getting ready, before you left for the beach, everyone loaded in their numbers." I started to send Summer a message and Brenna pushed my hand away from the phone.

"I want to give you your other gift." She got up and went over to the counter and picked up the black canvas. Brenna turned, rolling out some gold filament from a ball of twine. She started wrapping it around a red tipped black feather. When it was twined around the stem she placed the filament on the square. "What is that?" Curious, I moved closer. Joining the black feather and the gold filament were some herbs.

"This is your charm for your transition." She pointed to each herb, "Comfrey for safety while traveling, jasmine for prophetic dreams, mint for energy and keeping a clear head, and a bay leaf for protection." I noticed there was a drawing on the bay leaf of a blackbird with a twig in its mouth. "The feather I found lying outside our back door this morning. As you know, the blackbird is your father's, or an Elemental's, totem. When I saw this lying by the back door, it may or may not have been his intent, but I thought that its power would be helpful to you and hoped that you could possibly draw energy from it as you transitioned tonight."

I gingerly picked up the black canvas charm. Brenna handed me some more of the gold filament and I tied it into a knot. I looped it over my head and it came to rest on my chest. I breathed in the scent of bergamot and cinnamon, now mixed lightly with the mint from my charm. Those scents, mixed with the lavender coming in through the open window, calmed me. I closed my eyes and let the moment of quiet wash over me as the sun set. With it, a sense of rightness swept through me. I opened my eyes and looked at my aunt. I thanked her with a small smile and a hug and went to my room to think.

Brenna was right, my mom wouldn't care about anything but my being safe, but I knew I could trust my friends to help me out. I thought of Cole and Devon and frowned slightly. Cole had been my friend since I arrived in Dover, teaching me how to defend myself and giving me some pretty good advice. He had trained from a pretty young age to look out for me, to be my Guardian. I was sure that I could trust him. I fingered the necklace he'd given me last night, which had been a complete contradiction to the way that he'd been acting lately. With the exception of the dance last night, he'd been almost standoffish.

When my thoughts turned to Devon, I blushed slightly and my ring started to warm. I touched it with my other hand and then put that hand under my leg, sitting on it and trying to ignore the sensation. He and I had gotten so close in so little time. I thought of what his father wanted from him and gave a small shiver. I no longer had any doubts, I knew I could trust him. His father wanted to give him, body and soul, over to Avdar. There's no way he'd go along with that! I picked up my cell phone to send him a text, when it dinged before I could type anything.

COLE: R U there?
ME: Hey! Got my new phone!
COLE: Cool. Will u meet me @ school? Soccer field?

ME: Sure. When?
COLE: Now? I'm there already.
ME: What's up?
COLE: I have something else to give u b4 tonight.
ME: okay! See u soon!

I borrowed Brenna's car and promised to be home by 11 p.m. when we were all meeting up. I drove into the parking lot at school and pulled into a spot next to Cole's car. I looked towards the soccer field and saw a light flick on and off. I wasn't too thrilled with coming out here at night on my own. Everyone was meeting over at my house at 11 to get ready. Brenna had finished the charms to help everyone enter my transition spiritually with me. This little side trip of Cole's was kind of unexpected, and well, with everything that has been going on lately, didn't seem too smart. I took out my phone and shot a quick text to Devon and Summer, letting them know I was at the school. I turned off my phone, got out of the car, and started walking out towards the soccer field.

The light flicked on again, and I realized that Cole had the flashlight app on his phone turned on so I could see where he was. I reached for my phone and flicked that light on to flash it at Cole. As I did, it dinged with a message from Summer asking me what Cole wanted. I sent her back a quick note that I'd just gotten here and then silenced my phone.

"Cole?" My voiced seemed loud in the darkness, and I heard a rustle coming from the light. I stopped when I heard a groan. I tilted my head, staring at the light, and heard the groan again. "Cole!" Anxiously, I rushed forward as I saw a figure lying on the ground. I kneeled down next to it and turned the body over. Blonde, not brown, hair caught the light from the phone and illuminated Devon's face. My breath caught when I saw the cut above his right eye and the blood dripping down the side of his face into his hairline.

"Devon!" I touched his face, and shook his shoulder gently trying to wake him. He groaned again and opened his eyes. "Devon, what happened? What are you doing here?" I asked anxiously and he blinked as if trying to focus. He tried to sit up too quickly, groaned again and put his hand to his head. I helped him remain sitting and got a napkin out of my bag and touched it to the cut, dabbing at it. He pushed my hand away and looked around quickly.

"Avery, why are we on the soccer field?" He asked in confusion. When he started getting to his feet I stood as well but kept my hand on his arm. I looked around too. The field was completely dark, except for a phone lying on its side at Devon's feet.

I bent down to grab the phone and told him about Cole's text asking me to meet him here. "I did think it was kind of weird. I mean, no one's around, but he said he had something to give me," I said in defense when he gave me a look.

Devon took the phone from me and looked at it. "This isn't mine, it's Cole's." He scrolled through the text messages and we saw the text that was sent to me.

"What are you doing here?" I asked him, and at my words, he looked confused for a moment.

"The last thing I remember was driving to my house. From the bump on my head, I'd say that someone brought me here for some reason," he said starting to look angry.

"Do you think it was Cole? I did see his car in the parking lot." I said and I looked back toward the lot but couldn't see much. In the darkness, though, I did think I saw movement. Scared, I grabbed Devon's arm again and turned him toward it. “Look!” I pointed back towards the edge of the field. “I think I see something moving over there,” I said.

Even though I was trying to turn him towards what I was seeing, he was standing unmoving, looking over my shoulder at the other side of the field. “I do too, over there,” he said, pointing behind me.

I turned in the other direction, quickly, and saw a couple of dark shapes moving closer. I called out, “Cole?”

I wasn’t shocked when there wasn’t an answer. I looked around us and I could see more shapes gathering. Devon fiddled with the phone in his hand and the flashlight turned back on illuminating four figures standing with us at their center. They weren’t Daïmonids, but they were men I didn’t recognize. A figure stepped forward from behind one of the men and I recognized Cole.

“Cole?” I questioned in relief. “Who are all of these people?” I gestured around us. Cole’s gaze darkened and he looked at me with regret.

“I’m sorry Avery, but the Sentinel has decided that the risk is too big to allow you to fully transition tonight.” Turning to look at Devon, he continued, “and the power you two have together may be a danger to all Others.” He took an angry step forward.

I felt Devon grab my hand and try to push me behind him slightly, but I wouldn’t allow it. “My Father decided this?” Shocked, I shook off Devon’s hand. “He’s decided that I’m going to turn on the Elementals? Why? What have I done to show that I would harm anyone?” I said angrily. I felt a pang in my chest, realizing that my own father, and one of my best friends, could think so little of me.

“And you? You believe this too?” I glared at him, and he swallowed hard, looking torn. “Is that why you’ve been acting all weird lately?" I reached up and pulled the necklace he'd given me out of my shirt. "Why even bother to give me this?" I said wanting to tear the necklace off and throw it in his face, but I didn't. I tucked it back into my sweater.

At that gesture, Cole's face softened. He ignored all but my first question, answering, "I hate to think you would harm anyone, but he's the Sentinel, and as a Guardian, I must obey my orders." As he finished talking, he stood a little straighter, as if at attention.

"Those orders being...?" I asked, and felt Devon start to pull energy towards him. He grabbed my hand again, and this time, I let him. When our rings met and started to warm, I pushed my hurt away and focused on the two of us surviving.

Cole took a step forward, his hands clenched at his side, "You can't transition," he said bluntly.

Suddenly, I understood. The only way for me to not transition is for me to no longer be alive. To live was to move forward, turning sixteen, and everything that comes with that. If I died, my powers died with me. I felt Devon lean towards me and whisper, "It's 11:45." Already? I knew what he was telling me. I had only fifteen minutes before my transition. Headlights from the parking lot behind me illuminated Cole's face and I read his intent, just as I heard three car doors shut with a loud bang.

At that distraction, Devon threw a fireball towards a man to our left, encasing him in fire. At the man's screams, Cole gave a frustrated look and flung a hand out towards a sprinkler that was just to the right of him, and it turned on, dousing the flames.

I turned forward to face Cole with Devon at my side, our hands joined. "Are you sure you want to do this Cole?" I asked, hoping that he would have a change of heart. But seeing his determined expression, I knew that he would follow his orders. "Well, Happy Birthday to me," I said darkly as I felt our joined power thrum through my body. I could hear footsteps running up behind us and I threw up a protective shield for my friends. Seeing the electricity breakers on a pole next to them, I directed a blast to fling open that large metal box.

"Summer turn on the lights!" I shouted over my shoulder, and heard a couple of steps, then the lights slowly started to go on.

"Avery, what's going on?" Summer asked and I heard the frustration and fear in her voice. "I got your text and have everything here with us." I heard Summer's growl from the edge of the field and she murmured something and then Ben's voice.

"Cole, what the hell are you doing? Avery's cool!" Ben yelled and I could hear him pacing frantically behind the shield.

Cole, when the others ran up, looked resigned, then even more determined. "No. No she isn't cool. She is a danger to everybody! A danger to all of you!" He yelled at Ben, and his eyes started to glow a vibrant purple as he pulled energy out of the earth around him. Grass shriveled and died where he stood, and a giant mound of dirt started growing, lifting him up high.

"Shit, he's gone crazy!" I heard Ben say to Summer behind me and her murmured agreement.

"Avery, you've got to take this field down, we can help." Ana's voice came from farther down the stands, as she tested the boundaries of the field.

"No. This is my fight." I said quietly, looking Cole in the eyes, seeing that spark of friendship, and maybe something that could've been more, die. That hope in my heart died right along with it. I felt a hand grip mine and felt the warmth of a different, stronger kind of friendship grow. A friendship based upon truth, not lies. A friendship that would last through all of this pain and be stronger when it was all over.

"It's our fight." Devon corrected me and I broke eye contact with Cole to look at him.

"Are you sure?" My hair was starting to whip around my face, and I could see Devon's eyes had turned an arctic blue. A dust devil started to swirl gently in front of us, and then grew larger. My heart filled with a new hope.

"Absolutely!" He gave me a quick smirk and then whipped his free hand out to the side. The dust devil grew to the size of a baseball diamond, pushing Cole and his men back a few yards, until Cole flung his own power at it and held it back. It swirled in front of him, picking up dried grass and twigs. Through that whirlwind, I saw Cole reach up to his eyebrow and touch a finger to the piercing. With a loud crack a lightning bolt ripped from the sky into the middle of the tornado, dispersing it and causing Devon and me to duck to escape the debris. I saw his hand reach up again, and I took a step away from Devon. Cole tracked me with his eyes, and then whipped his hand out towards me and shot power directly at me. I released a blast of energy from my owns hands and my soft green power hit his purple ray of energy and deflected it to the right, into one of Cole's men, who dropped to the ground, dead. I gasped in horror at that strike but had to recover quickly.

I saw the other men look at each other, and then gather closer to Cole who stepped toward us. "Nice. I see you learned something from our lessons. It's too bad I didn't have time to teach you some offensive maneuvers," he said as he smirked. I froze in horror as I realized why our lessons had never progressed further.

"That's why she has me!" Devon angrily said from beside me and shot a blaze of fire toward Cole hitting him in the side. Cole stumbled to one knee and sent a bolt of purple energy at Devon. I stepped in front of him with my shield, defusing the hit. Devon stepped to the side, a storm gathering in the air directly overhead. Rain started pouring down over two of Cole's men, who screamed in pain, their skin turning a bright red and then bursting into blisters their skin melting from their hands. They dissolved into a dark pile of sludge. Cole glanced toward them and raised an eyebrow in disgust at Devon.

"That acid rain is a bitch," Devon said evenly. I looked over at him in shock and then my whole body contracted in pain when I took a bolt of energy in the side.

I fell to the ground but covered myself with a shield while holding my hand over the wound. Devon took my hand and sent a warm current of power through me. That power circulated through the wound in my side, easing the pain. I struggled to stand up into a crouch. Cole had one remaining man standing at his side, although he looked like he had second thoughts about being there.

I flicked my fingers at him sending a bolt of energy into the ground at his feet, and sure enough, he turned around and ran. I felt proud when Cole stared after his man and frowned in disgust. He turned around, his grey hoodie blending in with the ash-colored dirt around him I prepared myself for the next round. Cole whipped his hands out to the side and screamed, and a loud crack of thunder answered his call.

Together, Devon and I joined hands, siphoning energy from Cole and the storm he was building. Cole strained to gather power to him, but Devon and I were too strong. I stepped forward as far as Devon would let me, without separating our hands, feeling the power blazing into my body, with Devon as a conduct. The two of us were surrounded by light.

"Cole. Stop." I whispered. I had to try, one more time to reach him. My hand stretched toward him, beseechingly. "Please, let's stop this before we really hurt each other." He looked at me with sorrow in his eyes.

"Avery, it's my duty. My family, my father, he's counting on me," he said, the tone of his voice telling the agony of his decision. "I really liked you. I'm sorry." As he finished his sentence he shoved both hands towards me throwing all of that power that he'd built up from the storm, into my body, and I arched back with a cry.

He didn't realize what I could do, I realized, or he'd never have sent me all of his power. It swept through my body, a raging fire, and I siphoned most of the power into Devon. But, I held some of it back. I stared into Cole's eyes, my back arched, I kept drawing power from him, siphoning it into Devon, while my mind flashed back to visions of the first day I saw Cole, laughing at our training sessions, that shiver of awareness when his teeth grazed my neck at the dance, and that final kiss. Cole's features went white, his purple eyes wide in shock as he stared in disbelief. "What, how is it possible?" He stopped speaking abruptly, eyes fading to a pale lavender and fell onto the ground, still.

Devon squeezed my hand, his eyes burning bright blue, "Avery, we need to disperse this, it's too much!" He yelled anxiously.

I nodded, the rush of power giving me vertigo. I closed my eyes pulled the power back from Devon and fed it back to the earth but holding some of it in reserve. The grass on the soccer field grew lush and thick, bright yellow dandelions and mustard flowers sprouted and then bloomed, blossoms covering the field. The stadium lights flickered once and went out.

In the sudden darkness, I collapsed to my knees on the ground sobbing and crawled over to Cole.

"Cole. Cole. Wake up!" I shook him, not wanting it to be true. I turned him over so I could pat his face. "Come on. You need to wake up!" I cried, my tears falling on him as I leaned over his body, hugging his chest. I felt Devon standing next to me and our friends gathered around in quiet shock. I put my hands on his chest and concentrated, then sent a pulse of earth energy into Cole's chest. His back arched, and then his body slumped back to the ground. I did it again. I could hear Ana crying softly and Summer knelt down next to me, wrapping an arm around my shoulder her head on my neck.

Devon touched my shoulder and then leaned down to feel for Cole's pulse. "Avery, stop. He's gone." he said quietly, regret in his voice.

I shook my head in denial. I couldn't believe that this whole thing just happened. My father set my friend against me. Unable to express how I was feeling, I grew silent, my sobs quieting until I felt only anger.

I heard Ben murmur something in Summer's ear and her arm tightened around my shoulder.

"What time is it?" I asked. My voice tremored slightly from the emotions I was holding back.

"It's 11:59." Ana answered quickly. I glanced at her and could barely make out her shape in the darkness but saw her reach a hand up to wipe away her tears. I looked at everyone. Tear-filled eyes met mine. I swiped a hand under my own and looked towards Summer. Ben looked at Cole's body and then away, his jaw set.

"We're out of time, you guys. Summer, you said you brought everything?" She nodded, putting her hand in the bag that hung from her shoulder. "We need to get ready," I said wearily and I pushed against the lush grass as I got up.

"Brenna told you what we needed to do?" I asked Summer and she nodded, handing out the black velvet pouches, and a few vials of liquid. She took out four foil sheets, the type you used for emergency blankets, and set them in a square around Avery.

"Avery, you need to sit in the middle. Everyone else, sit on one of the foil sheets. Avery you are going to enter your spiritual transition, as planned. The rest of us will chant this spell as you enter it. Brenna said it was a pretty simple spell, so our spirits should immediately follow." She handed out four sheets of paper. I looked down at it blankly, then felt them watch me settle onto the ground at their center.

As I closed my eyes, I could feel the group gather around me. I took a breath, determined to find my focus and made a vow that I would mourn Cole later. I pushed everything that just happened aside, took another deep breath and let it out gently. I took another breath, focusing inward, and the golden light within me expanded and grew. My whole body felt light, and a gentle wind stirred. As I focused on that light, I noticed it was rimmed in lavender, part of Cole's essence remaining with me.

Chapter 29

Devon

As Avery settled into the middle of our group, the rest of us gathered on our foil sheets. Everyone avoided looking at Cole's body lying a few feet away. I looked directly at Summer seated directly across from me and saw her mouth something at Ben, who wiped his eyes, nodded and quickly looked down at the ground. I closed my eyes, just as a warm golden light surrounded Avery.

I gripped the paper in one hand, looking down at the words. In my other hand I held the vial of liquid. I heard Summer's voice start chanting the first line and the rest of us quickly joined in. I hoped Cole's death wouldn't affect the power of Brenna's spell.

In unison we started.

We are five Champions of earth,

Summer:

I am the Champion of spirit,

Ana:

I am the Champion of sight,

Ben:

I am the Champion of touch,

Me:

I am the Champion of intent,

For Cole's part we all chanted:

I am the Champion of security.

We all spoke together:

We offer our talents
A gift for this night
With our spirits a transforming sight
Follow the glow that we see alight.

Send our spirits to the transforming dream
Follow the light to give Avery the means
Send our spirits to the powerful scene
Follow the light of Avery's dream

As we said the last sentence a loud crack and flash of light had my eyes flying open in surprise. I found myself sitting on the ground, surrounded by my sister, Dani, and several Daïmonids.

Shocked I slowly got to my feet, my knees creaking as I stood up. My sister leaped over to me and gave me a quick hug.

"Hey!" She took a step away, almost skipping in glee. I looked quickly around, trying to see where Summer, Ben and Ana were, but only saw the Daïmonids standing next to a small grouping of rocks in a clearing of Eucalyptus trees. A few of the leaves were twirling in the wind as they floated to the ground on a breeze.

I nodded at my sister and brushed my hands off on my jeans. I decided to pretend that I had meant to arrive here with them and asked, "Are we in Avery's dream transition?" I quickly made a head count of how many Daïmonids were with my sister and took two steps back towards the water running in the brook behind me.

Dani nodded yes to my question and then squinted her eyes at me briefly. "When you weren't home to cross with me, I was worried you were backing out." She said quickly, then raced forward and grabbed my hand. "I'm so glad you made the right decision!" She twirled in a circle in front of me, skipping forward on the path.

I tugged slightly on my hand and she let it go. "So, what's the plan?" I smiled at my sister hoping I projected innocence.

"Well, if you hadn't been avoiding us, you'd know." She swung an arm wide, indicating the Daïmonids with her. "These guys are going to help us capture Avery's power." She started walking away, up a path that ran beside the brook.

"Have you seen Avery yet?" I asked, starting to walk slowly behind her, looking around again. I didn't see Summer, Ben, and Ana anywhere. Did my sister somehow interfere with our spell? At this point, I was just going to worry about myself, and then Avery once we found her. It's time to make nice with my sister until that happens. I quickened my steps and slung an arm around Dani's shoulder.

"So what did you say the plan was?" She gave me a sideways look and then smiled.

Chapter 30

Avery

I closed my eyes and took a deep breath in as far as I could, my chest burning slightly, then slowly let the air release from my lungs, easing the strain. I did it again, then again, and focused on the golden light within me. As I focused on the light I heard the distant chant of my friends and the light expanded until behind my eyes there wasn't darkness, only light.

I opened my eyes, surprised to find myself standing in a wooded area next to a stream. My mouth dry, I looked around and then knelt to dip a hand in the water to take a drink. The water was very cold, yet a warm wind blew lightly, dispelling the chill. A piece of my hair blew into my eyes and I reached up to push the strand behind my ears and caught the sound of bells jingling. I looked around for the source of the sound but didn't find anything. Thinking it might be coming from across the stream, I stepped up to the edge. I saw a few stones that made a path and stepped from one to the other until I reached the other side. The sun lit up a pathway that led through the thin trunks of Aspen trees. As I walked along I heard a rustling in the shrubs to my left. Without thought, I drew an arrow from the quiver on my back and pointed it towards the noise. In surprise, I looked down at the bow in my hands, then shrugged, pulling the arrow back. I sighted on a very large blackbird that flew out from the middle of the shrub. Remembering the red tipped feather in my charm, I lowered my arrow. The sun glinted off the purple quartz arrowhead and cast a lavender light on the ground in front of me. I thought immediately of the necklace Cole had given me last night and reached up to touch it with a smile. I wasn't surprised it had disappeared. I touched my finger to the arrowhead that looked remarkably like the pendant on the gift Cole gave me and as I looked at the arrowhead, it faded away, the bow and quiver also disappearing from my back. *Interesting*, I thought. The blackbird caught my eye again stepping into the light and as we stared at each other I wondered if I wasn't being stupid to trust a blackbird. I mean, my father and his people could turn into blackbirds. I looked into this blackbird's little black eye and saw a glint of green light. As I stared at that green light, I heard a voice speak a word. I jumped slightly, looking around. No, I was alone. I looked at the bird again, and again, I heard a voice, speak just one word.

"Follow." The bird tilted its head at me in a questioning manner. I nodded. *Okay*, I thought, *why not? I'm supposed to have my friends here with me, but until that happens, I might as well see what this little guy wants.* I started walking forward and the bird flew before me down the path. I followed its flight into a clearing where I saw two women waiting for me. The blackbird landed on the shoulder of the younger woman, who I immediately recognized. I couldn't believe it! I ran ahead, my eyes intent on her, hoping she wouldn't disappear before I got there.

"Mom!" I shouted excitedly. My mother put up a hand stopping me before I reached her. "Is it really you?" I asked, panting lightly from my run. My mother looked exactly like she did the day she died. She was wearing the same pair of black jeans, boots and cranberry crew neck sweater that she had on that day at breakfast. Her softly curling brown hair hung to mid shoulder, and her brown eyes were focused intently on mine. I wanted to reach out and hug her, tell her how much I missed her, but by the look on her face, she wasn't here to say hi and catch up.

"Avery, I'm so happy to see you looking so well." She smiled quickly, but then frowned, looking down the path behind me. "I wish we had time to talk, but we need you to focus on what we're going to tell you." She motioned to the older woman beside her, "Avery this is my mother, your grandmother, Vivian."

I drew in a breath in shock, "The prophetess." I exhaled. I wanted to move towards her and give her a big hug too, but instead reached my hand out to hers in a lame gesture to shake hands. "Umm, hi Grandma, umm, Vivian?" As my hand neared hers, she reached up to halt my action.

"Avery, we are here in spirit only." As she said this, my hand passed right through hers. I waved my hand around a little, then let it drop to my side in disappointment. "Okay. What are you guys doing here?" I looked around the clearing, checking to see if Devon or any of my friends had shown up. No one was in sight.

Not waiting for a response to my question, I blurted out, "Mom, did you know Dad was going to try to have the Elementals kill me? One of my best friends just died, trying to follow Dad's orders!" I looked at her accusingly, my heart breaking again when I thought of Cole dying.

My mom looked down at the ground in disappointment, "I had hoped that I was wrong." She shook her head slightly and then stood up a little straighter. "I hadn't heard from him in over a year. He had started to change so much when he was made Sentinel. When I'd call to check in, I could hear the distance in his voice and hear the lies he spoke. He always asked questions about you and if you'd started to show any signs of powers. Not how you were doing or what you were doing in school." Her voice sounded so disappointed, and when she looked at me, she was sad.

While my mother was giving me the lowdown on my scummy father, I noticed my grandmother, Granny? Vivian? I mentally shrugged. Anyway, I noticed my Gran looking down at my ring. I reached over and gave it a twist. She nodded, looking pleased.

"Gran, I can call you Gran, right?" At my question my Gran nodded, looking pleased. I guess I got that moniker right, at least. "Gran, I found out a lot about this ring. My friend Devon and his sister Dani have two that are very similar."

My Gran nodded, and then answered the question I had been thinking. "Yes, Gaea took part in that event because she didn't want Atticus and Flora Finn to gain all of that power. One family with too much power would have been an imbalance in our world," she said.

I nodded, and asked uncertainly, "Isn't that kind of why everyone's out to get me though? They think that after tonight I will have too much power?" I asked, sounding worried. My mother became angry, and my Gran looking very formidable, denying that statement.

"When I foresaw your birth, I did say that you would have tremendous power, but what everyone is forgetting, is that I said that you could become destructive to Others, but I also said that you could become our savior." She looked at my mother in anger. "I just don't understand how that second part got left off of the prophecy?" Her frustration was very clear in that last statement.

Hearing this, I felt a surge of confidence. I wasn't going to automatically become this evil being! The sky brightened to a robin's egg blue, and each blade of grass reached towards me and grew impossibly green. A flock of blackbirds flew out of the aspens and dove through the sky gaily. My right hand started to sweat from the heat generating from my ring finger. My Gran smiled and her eyes twinkled with pride, and then she joined hands with my mother.

"Your mother and I, although very happy to see you, have only a few more moments. In our family, when our women go through our transitions, we bless our newest Seer with her gifts personally. We need you to kneel please." She said, motioning at the ground.

I knelt down in front of my Mom and Gran and looked up at them with blurred vision. One tear escaped and rolled down my right cheek. Their joined hands hovered over my head and as I looked down towards the ground, I felt their hands warmth touch me and spread through my whole body. The warmth grew until it was rushing through my veins in a wave of energy. My vision hazed over, and looking up again, I saw my Mom and Gran each put a hand to their lips and start to fade away.

In a rush, I leapt to my feet and moved my body forward until it was merged with the fading image of them. I felt a brief touch, and my heart and body filled with light. "I love you honey," was a whisper in my ear. Then they were gone.

Alone and feeling that love and that rush of power that they gave me, a power that was blessed and good, I gave a laugh and spun in a circle. Power trickled out of my hands and swirled around me in streaks of green and gold. Butterflies dodged through those waves and fluttered through the yellow flowers dotting the clearing.

Dizzy, I sat abruptly on the ground, breathing heavily. So, what happens now? I don't know what kind of powers I have earned. Except for feeling buzzed, I felt the same as I did before. I mentally shrugged. *I guess I'll find out when I need to*, I thought. Looking around, I got to my feet. My friends hadn't arrived, and I wasn't sure Brenna's spell would actually work, although she seemed to be really confident that it would.

I started back towards the path that I had used to enter the clearing when Dani and Devon, arm in arm, stepped out of the trees. A few crows flew down out of the tree behind them and Daïmonids popped into existence. Glancing around, I counted six of them, all wearing their signature sunglasses.

The wind stilled and the sky darkened. Clouds shifted across the sun, casting the meadow in shadow. Devon, glancing at the darkening sky, withdrew his arm from Dani's and stepped forward. I was horrified as I looked between the two of them. At my look, Devon shook his head and widened his eyes and I relaxed slightly. His pace quickened until he was almost running up the path towards me. Still unsure, I flicked my hand out to the left, halting Devon about three feet in front of me. Dani walked slowly up the path until she stopped next to her brother. The Daïmonids fanned out behind her. I felt the weight of the quiver appear on my back and reached for an arrow. As I pulled it over my shoulder, it grew in length until I held an amethyst tipped spear in my hand.

"Devon, what's going on?" I asked, my voice quavered with accusation. He tilted his head towards his sister and took a step away from her. As he did, he brought up his hand with the ring on it and placed it against my shield.

"Avery, we aren't here to hurt you. We're here to help." He said raising an eyebrow and gave me a brief smile, taking his hand off my shield and facing his sister. "Well, at least I am!" He exclaimed and shot a pulse of power at Dani, catching her off guard and pushing her off her feet. She did a neat backwards flip and landed facing forward, a look of fury on her face.

I phased the shield so that it shimmered, just in front of him, and let him step through it. He reached out and grabbed my hand, giving me a quick hug. "Where did you meet up with her?" I asked quickly, moving us back, trapping Dani and her Daïmonids on the other side. We quickly moved up the path, back towards the clearing I had just come from.

"We were chanting the spell, and I saw a flash of light. All of a sudden I was sitting on the ground in front of Dani and her buddies over there." He looked back over his shoulder and I followed his gaze where I could see his sister using her power to fling stones and dig trenches at and around the wall. The Daïmonids had taken off their sunglasses and were using their red laser gazes to try to burn through my shield.

I could feel a pressure building up in my head, and I shook it slightly, as if I could shake it off and make the pressure go away. I stumbled, and Devon grabbed hold of my arm, hurrying me up the path. "Where is everybody else?" I asked.

"I couldn't tell you, I've been stuck with them," he pointed over his shoulder "and we've been following that brook for a while." I felt a sharp pain in my head and picked up my pace.

"They're through my shield." We stopped pretty close to where I had the conversation with my mother and Gran, and I saw light hit something on the ground. Kneeling down, I picked up a marble sized sphere of black glass. *How odd*, I thought and shoved it into the pocket of my jeans.

"Did you find out their plans while you were trying to find me?" I asked Devon curiously. He was facing Dani and the Daïmonids, who were quickly coming up the path.

"It's the same old story, we are supposed to somehow steal your powers, and then when we get back home, they are going to hand me over to Avdar in some sort of ceremony, I guess? They obviously haven't given me a lot of details." He gripped his hands in frustration. He turned to look at me, his eyes changing color from cobalt to a light ice blue. "I think we are going to have to take a stand here." He said grimly.

"I agree." I said and I turned back around to see that Dani and the Daïmonids were just breaching the clearing. I drew in a breath and focused on the elements around me. This connection with my power was new, I felt every blade of grass turn in my direction. The wind gently ran its fingers through my hair.

"Can you feel that?" I asked as I held Devon's hand, our rings touching. I felt his anger and fire race through me and I gave him a little of my power back and felt him jerk. I turned to look at him and saw his hair standing on end and his blue eyes narrowed in concentration.

"Maybe back the power down a bit, Avery," he said between clenched teeth.

Hurriedly, I pulled my power back slightly until his hair stopped waving wildly, and his eyes turned a more normal blue. I smiled at him when he squeezed my hand in thanks. "Sorry." I said sheepishly.

Suddenly Summer, Ben, and Ana stepped out of the trees behind us. Relieved, I smiled and called out to them. Summer whooped, high fiving Ben. Ana, her freckles spinning madly, smiled slightly as her skin faded to an ash brown color, blending in with the bark of the trees behind her. I squeezed Devon's hand and pointed in their direction.

"Things have evened up a little bit." I grinned at him and looked over at my friends. "What took you guys so long?"

"Ave, you have no idea." Summer shook her long blonde hair over her shoulders and then started shifting. Her pink tipped nails grew longer, and she yawned, showing off her large fangs. She rotated her arms, loosening up her shoulders. She was inches taller, and her tail whipped out behind her, the tip twitching back and forth.

Ben, his skin already a slightly green hue, smiled and zapped his tongue out to snag a fly. He looked behind us at Dani and the Daïmonids, tilted his head to the side and cracked his neck. He chewed on the fly calmly. He shrugged out of his jacket and then his body just started growing and turning a vivid green. He kept his focus behind us, not saying anything. He frowned and moved up on Devon's other side.

I looked at Ana, slightly worried.

She nodded calmly and then spoke, "When we came into your transition, we were on the other side of the meadow," she said. "I camouflaged myself and heard some of their plans." She looked at Devon. "Dani is supposed to distract you while everyone else focuses on Avery. The plan is to keep you separate, but safe, so that your body," and she shrugged apologetically, "is okay for when Avdar takes it over."

I felt Devon tense up next to me and gave him a pat on the shoulder. "We're not going to let him get near you," I promised and he nodded.

I gave Ana a grateful smile. She wasn't a warrior, but she did have skills and shouldn't be underestimated.

Remembering Ana's training from her father I said, "Why don't you step over by those boulders, and blend in. Feel free to yell out directions or see anything we need to know." I said, pulling the bow and arrows that had again mysteriously appeared on my back out and handed them to her.

"I'm guessing you know how to use these?" She nodded, giving the string a quick tug.

"Yeah." At my raised eyebrow, she murmured "My dad." With the bow in hand, she climbed onto the first boulder, her skin fading until I couldn't see her anymore.

"Great." I turned back around and stepped back up to Devon. Totally confident, "Let's do this.

Chapter 31

Devon

I had been ignoring my sister, her screams of frustration increasing when she couldn't immediately break through the shield. Suddenly, I felt the pop as Avery's shield collapsed under the combined force of the Daïmonid's laser gaze and Dani's pummeling it with boulders and rocks.

In the past, my sister's temper had made her dangerous, but also impulsive. When you are impulsive you make mistakes. As I stared across the meadow at her, we locked eyes. I concentrated on that piece of me that was linked to her and tried to feel for her thoughts. She had always been more eager to please our father, but I never thought that she would betray me like this. Looking into those ice blue eyes, I suddenly remembered an incident from our childhood.

I looked up from my meditation when the door to the library swung open. My grandmother had me practice meditation every day to help focus my thoughts. I now had total control and wouldn't mesmerize anyone by accident, but I had liked the quiet of the library, so continued the practice.

My sister stood in the doorway. At twelve she was still small for her age. It frustrated her, because she wanted the power and strength that came with size, but eventually she learned to use her smallness to her advantage. She was willful and hated when our father wouldn't look beyond her petite height but learned quickly to play on her femininity and strike coy poses. My father usually saw through that act, but other people bought into it, and she usually got what she wanted. That coyness didn't work on me, though. As her twin, I knew the strength that resided within her, and the fact that she had power over an element? Right there, that showed her fortitude. Our lessons were nothing to scoff at; we spent hours honing our skills. Dani was stronger at wielding Earth than most boys her age. That also pleased my father a lot.

Movement at my side had me glancing down and reaching out a hand to stroke over wiry gray fur. The dog growled slightly, nuzzling into my side.

She glanced at her dog and I saw a look of anger cross her face, until she wiped it clear. I gave the dog a pat, then shrugged at my sister. I hadn't meant to charm him, but it was kind of nice to have him around.

Dani walked over to the chair beside me and flung herself down. One leg slung over an arm of the chair.

"What are you doing?" She had grass stains on the knees of her pants and dirt under her nails. I could tell she had been out playing in the yard again, practicing on her own. It's been a long time since I was allowed any free time. Handling three elements put a lot of pressure on me.

Dani also got her power a couple of weeks ago on our twelfth birthday. She is the only girl to have gotten this power in over a century. That combined with my own three, and the Mesmer powers, elevated our fathers' position within Elemental society. In my eyes, this was a good thing, because he was gone a lot more at various meetings and wasn't around to harass me. I think Dani missed him though.

"I'm practicing." She looked at Pebble again, then quickly away, biting her lip.

"I said I was sorry!" I blurted out, and she nodded once sharply, her blue gaze darkening.

"I know." She reached forward again. Pebble had been her dog before I accidentally mesmerized him. The dog scooted away from her huddling behind my knees with a soft growl. She frowned and then looked towards the window.

I stroked the dog's back again, wishing I could return the love of her pet. I didn't blame her for still being unhappy that her dog wouldn't go near her anymore, but well, she needed to get over it. I saw her straighten her spine and when she glanced at me again. Her eyes had turned their normal lighter shade of blue. I leveled my gaze on her, curious, and reached out with my mind, but came up against a wall. I concentrated on that wall, trying to reach beyond it to find out what she was feeling.

My sister was always testing me. She said it was for practice, but I think she wanted to best me. I was more talented, and if she could intimidate me into a reaction and misuse my abilities she'd be able to report to my father. I prepared myself.

My hand lifted slightly off my knee, my fingers undulating slightly. Our gazes clashed. My hand tightened into a fist. Dani's hand, resting in her lap, also tightened into a fist. She swung her leg off the arm of the chair and sat up straight. Staring into her eyes, I could feel our gazes lock in with a snap. She still had that wall up, so this time I focused inward. Maybe there was a way to break down her wall, but by using the tie of life energy we had, as twins. I'd created a safe spot in my mind that I could mentally escape to when my father was being especially difficult. It looked like the room I was sitting in, with a fire burning and the chair I was sitting in next to the fire. But this room was in my mind. The library in my mind was not only a safe place, but a room where I put the minds of those I wanted to mesmerize. I did not want to see my sister in that compartment, but it may be time to show her that I could put her there.

I hummed a tuneless melody, feeling the heat from the flames in the fireplace, as I drew on that energy, heating up the room. I kept humming, and fluttered my fingers, creating a wave of heat in the air between us. I focused on the room in my head, throwing that vision through that wave of heat, at the wall in Dani's mind.

She rocked back slightly, her pupils widening. I stopped the hum of sound and snapped my fingers. "Dani?" She sat staring straight ahead. Took a deep breath and then shuddered slightly. I'm not sure it worked, but she looked scared. Staring at me with wide eyes. I had told her to stop testing my powers. If I had wanted to, I could've captured her mind. I'd never do that, of course, she was my twin sister, but these games needed to stop.

I looked at the flames leaping in the fireplace, letting the heat wash over me, I opened my mouth to reassure her, but when I turned back to the chair across from me, she was gone.

Now, looking at her across that meadow, hearing Ana speak of their plans they'd made for me, I wondered if four years later, it was possible for me to take her out of this battle. If I could use my Mesmer powers, I wouldn't have to hurt her.

A flock of crows swooped out of the sky. I heard a quick succession of pops, and the meadow filled with Daïmonids, and at the center of them was Avdar. He grinned at me and then narrowed his gaze on Avery.

Keeping my eyes on them, I said out loud, so Avery could hear me, "I need to try to take my sister out of this. I would never forgive myself if I hurt her."

I could feel Avery looking at me, probably thinking of our battle with Cole, and the horror of his loss. She slowly nodded. "All right, if you think you can do that?" she asked, and I nodded.

She looked over at Summer and Ben. "Guys, we are seriously outnumbered. This isn't really your battle, so why don't you sit this one out."

A loud hiss came from Summer's direction and Ben gave a loud sound that was a cross between a war cry and a hiccup. I laughed, yeah, nice try. I moved away from Avery, nodding at my sister.

She nodded back and stepped to the right side of the meadow, away from the other Daïmonids, her blonde ponytail swinging behind her shoulders as she shook her head. "You need to get back in the game Devon. It's not too late for you to switch back to our side!"

"Who are you kidding Dani?" I said shaking my head at her and glared my disappointment. "Why would you think I'd agree to this mad plan?"

She looked shocked, which for some reason I found really funny. This was just like Dani. She always agreed with everything our father did, but never thought things through. "Dani, think. I won't be here anymore. Just my body." I pointed over at Avdar across the field, who was viewing the fight between the Daïmonids and Avery, Summer, and Ben. "He will be in my body. I, my soul, will not be in it anymore. I'll be gone!"

"Father says that this is the only way for our family to..."

"Yeah, right. It's the only way for our family to gain more status. He means him, not us. And do you really think that Avdar is going to go along with Father's plan?" Avdar had taken his attention away from us to watch Summer and Ben leap into action against a group of Daïmonids. I heard a few pops but focused on Dani.

"He has his own plans. Who knows what they are, besides world domination, I'm sure." This conversation was going nowhere. Dani was my father's tool. He had been honing her as a weapon against me for years, knowing that with her being my twin, I'd have trouble going up against her. True, but that didn't mean I couldn't take her out of the game.

I started gathering power from the sun, focusing on Dani's eyes. Before I could look inward to that room inside myself, I saw her eyes widen in horror. She sprinted towards me, and just as she was within arms distance, she leaped forward, pushing her hands against the earth, and doing a back flip over my head. Her ponytail brushed over my forehead and I whirled around to see her knock a Daïmonid flat.

"You don't touch him," she hissed, throwing a hand out and backhanding him, at the same time the earth moved behind him and he fell into a trench. She waved her hand and the earth closed over him with a shudder. She yelled at the other Daïmonids who had come closer, and they backed off. I heard a laugh, and glanced over at Avdar, who was looking at Dani approvingly.

She turned back around to face me, her back to the action. Looking over her shoulder, I saw Ben body slam into five Daïmonids, wrapping his arms around them, covering them with bright green goo. They collapsed, disintegrating, and he gave a loud croak, and leaped towards a new group that suddenly sprang into existence.

I heard a twang and saw a Daïmonid get hit by an arrow, but it didn't seem to slow him down. He focused his gaze on Summer, and she eluded the laser-like gaze. I heard Avery yell and toss some rocks to Summer who used her soccer skills to fly back with a scissor kick, kicking the rocks into the head of one of the Daïmonids. His head exploded with a pop, and his body followed.

Seeing they had the battle in hand, I refocused on my sister. I looked into her eyes again, this time seeing uncertainty. I drew power down from the sun. Feeling it surge inside me, I slowly reached a hand out to her and said her name. She looked at my hand and reached out her own. I gave a hum of approval and took a step towards her. I pushed my power out, filling the air around us with heat and focused my mind inward. Looking into her eyes, I imagined her in the compartment in my mind.

Mentally, I pushed through the wall she had built around her mind, her eyes widened, and it was then that she realized what I was doing. She stilled, tried to raise her hand to shield her eyes, but I was in front of her, and I captured both of her hands, humming tonelessly. I took that wall down, brick by brick, until I could see the small girl inside, huddling in a corner of her mind.

Humming, I pushed that warmth into her head, thinking, you're safe, you're in my care. Her eyes glazed and she lightly gripped my hand, and then that grip relaxed. That little girl that had been huddled into a scared ball in her own head was now in the compartment in my own mind. She was looking around curiously, at the fire that was gently blazing, and at the green armchair that looked exactly like the armchair in the library of our home. A book appeared on the table next to the chair, along with a cup of tea and a plate of cookies. The little girl stepped forward and sank down into that chair. When she did, a small gray dog rushed forward and leaped into her lap, curling up. She ran a hand over the back of the dog and sighed, relaxing deeper into the chair.

I've got you, I whispered into my mind, and she nodded. I took a breath and opened my eyes. Dani was still standing in front of me, but the expression in her eyes had changed. She now looked at me with a love that had been missing in her expression since we were very little. Before we had received our powers.

Chapter 32

Avery

Summer and Ben leaped into the battle, hissing and bellowing their cries. Summer slashed, kicked, and rolled, eliminating Daïmonids quickly. As fast as they popped out of existence, more replaced them.

Ben's strategy was to use the strength in his legs. After his leap, he would jump over the Daïmonids and approach them from behind. I saw him tap one on the shoulder, and then just wrap his hand around his neck and kill him with the essence that oozed off his skin. He had the same problem as Summer though, as quickly as he killed them, they were replaced with more Daïmonids.

I heard twang after twang and saw Daïmonids being hit with arrows that seemed to fly out of nowhere. As soon as they were hit, the Daïmonids would snap the end of the arrow off and continue with their fight. I did notice one that had been hit multiple times start to take on a purple hue. He lit up from within, then burst into lavender fire.

I yelled back towards the boulders, where Ana was shooting, "Hit your target three times!" I heard three quick twangs and saw another Daïmonid quickly burst into lavender flame. Those Daïmonids weren't replaced by new ones, leading me to believe that there was a connection between the amethyst arrowheads and the fact that they weren't coming back after being eliminated. I twirled around, not spotting any more amethyst lying around. I scoffed at myself. Come on Avery, like amethysts would just be laying around waiting for us to use them as weapons. What could I do? I looked around again and walked over to a pile of rocks.

I wrapped my fingers around one of the stones and as I touched it, the rock began to glow. I concentrated on the stone, making it heat up and glow brighter. Feeling more confident I slowly got to my feet, and as I did, the stones on the ground around me started floating in the air, taking on a warm purple hue. I pictured these stones hurtling towards the Daïmonids as projectiles, shooting through their bodies. As my vision faded, the hovering stones shot outward and hit the Daïmonids chests. I continued to propel these amethyst missiles, yelling for Ana to hit those same targets. We worked together rapidly taking out multiple Daïmonids.

I heard a screech, and saw Summer go flying backwards to hit the pile of boulders Ana was hiding against. Avdar stalked forward, his robes plastered against him as he pushed against the wind. Ben snuck up behind him, but as he raised a hand, Ben became trapped in a box. Frantically he beat against the sides of it and jumped up trying to push his way through the top. The box was sealed tight, not allowing Ben to escape his prison.

Devon stepped up next to me and I looked at him, while grabbing his hand. "Where's your sister?" I asked quickly, and Devon nodded over to a tree stump behind the battle, across the meadow. She was sitting quietly, looking out on the battle like she was watching a quiet historical movie. Her hand was slowly petting the air above her lap.

I raised a brow at Devon.

"I'll explain later, after we kick this guy's ass." Devon said without taking his eyes off Avdar, who was stalking towards us.

I threw up a shield, but Avdar blew right through it. Devon and I started funneling our power between us, sharing our abilities. We continued to try to distract Avdar and stop him from advancing.

I pictured some more boulders, with their amethyst light, and as they rose from the ground, I felt someone stop their movement, holding onto the power I had generated. It was as if a hand held them down, and I pushed upwards with my power to try to push by that hand.

Only one escaped, and it flew towards Avdar, missing him but landing at his feet. It exploded and created a small crater in the earth, making him take a step back. Arrows flew towards him in quick succession, the first one striking him in the chest, but the others struck a shield he flung up. He growled and looked towards the boulders.

I yelled, "Ana, get down, Go! Go!" Panicked, I watched Avdar throw a block of Earth power at the boulders, and they cracked and flew apart. I heard a scream, and then silence.

Summer, who had fallen against those boulders, now lay underneath the rubble. Ana was silent, and I could only hope that she was all right. Avdar had started advancing again. Devon and I used the pieces of rubble he had created, and started flinging them at him, one by one. I didn't have time to turn them into amethyst missiles, and they struck harmlessly. The wind picked up and plastered my shirt to my chest, also making my hair whip around my face. The stones kept dropping around him, and the meadow was pitted with holes, some of which started to fill up with water. I glanced at Devon and saw that he was sweating. I funneled power through my ring into his, and saw steam start to rise up from the holes. The water began boiling and spitting into the air. Avdar laughed, and stopped where he stood, about thirty yards away from us.

"She's a perfect match for us!" He smiled slightly, backed up and then flung himself across the trench of water to the other side, landing in a perfect roll. He stood up, and I gasped in horror. We were separated by only a few yards of grass and stone.

Devon and I, our hands still clasped and burning from the heat of our rings combining energy, breathed heavily. There didn't seem to be enough air. The wind that had been whipping our clothes and hair had calmed until it was completely still.

The meadow was enrobed in silence. The sounds of birds crying had died. We were alone with this mad Daïmon.

All of a sudden, I felt movement in my pocket. Just a slight twitch, and then an ice cold fire raced down my leg. I placed my left hand on top of the small lump in my pants and remember that Obsidian marble I had found where I had first seen my mother and Gran. It was ice cold against my leg. Cold with power. I placed my hand in my pocket, as Avdar started to speak.

"That was admirable." Avdar said as he looked at the devastation in the field. The grass, no longer green, was dry and yellow all of its life energy stored inside Devon and me. The ground was pitted with holes and stones. Amidst the rubble were black marks, where Daïmonids had been eliminated. Their energy leaving behind a scorch in the earth as they died.

Devon, still holding my hand, took a slight step in front of me and addressed Avdar. As he started speaking, his power flew into me with a whoosh and I stood dazed. I heard his voice in my head, speaking into my mind at the same time he spoke to Avdar. "I have a plan," his voice said. "I think I can trap Avdar using my Mesmer powers."

I gasped in horror. "No!" I said to him, gripping the back of his shirt as he stood in front of me.

"You need more time to grow. To learn your new powers." He said. "If I fail, I know you'll fight to get me back." He spoke with a cocky confidence that I had learned meant he wasn't going to listen to me.

There's a big problem with this plan, I thought. *I'm not sure what my powers even are, and who is going to help me learn how to use them?* "Devon, don't do this. Don't let him take you." I said anxiously, tears welling up in my eyes.

"*I will fight. I promise you!*" he thought at her. "Look at my eyes and you'll know if it's me, or Avdar," he said quickly.

Devon squeezed my hand, and I started to pay attention to what he was saying to Avdar. My grip on his hand tightened in horror.

"If I agree to go with you, to let you take my body, will you leave Avery alone?" My hand burned against Devon's and I glanced down, surprised they weren't glowing. All of a sudden, the pulsing power stopped. Devon dropped my hand and stood directly in front of Avdar.

I felt dizzy with all of this power rushing through me and didn't hear Avdar's reply. I raised my head, shaking it slowly, realizing what Devon had done. He had given me everything. All of his power, save the Mesmer talent that I couldn't take from him. He was sacrificing himself, and even as he gave himself to Avdar, he didn't give him an ounce of our power.

I shot forward, "Devon, no!" I tried to push my way around him, but stumbled, the cold fire in my leg an agony

I could no longer ignore. I went to one knee, reaching out to touch the back of his leg.

He looked back at me longingly, then squared his shoulders and stepped into Avdar.

With one hand to the ground, I pushed myself up while reaching into my pocket with my other hand to grab onto the obsidian marble. As I took it out of my pocket and transferred it to my right hand, it touched my ring. The combined power both cold and hot shot through me.

In a daze, I stared at Devon's back. His hand was flicking the air at his side. A warm haze filled the air between us. I heard him humming, and then lightning struck the earth with a crack. That haze turned into fire rushing between us, and Devon slowly turned around. Flames whipped up making his face glow red, his blonde hair gently moving with the heat.

His eyes were no longer blue, they were a bright orange red: Avdar's eyes were staring back at me from within Devon's body. I sobbed in disbelief. He failed!

I took a step back in horror.

"Stupid boy, to believe that I would give you up?" He chuckled, then frowned slightly. He flung a hand toward me and I stumbled from the push of air but didn't feel any heat or wetness. He looked at the ground and growled, trying to do something with his hands. Only a few small pebbles rose into the air and then dropped weakly back into the ground. He looked at the ring on his hands. It was now a dull lifeless nickel color, the vibrancy of its power, gone. He yelled and advanced towards me, reaching out. "You've stolen my power!" He raged.

He wrapped his hands around my neck and started to squeeze. The air left my lungs, but the power that was inside me rose up, Devon's power, and with a yell, I shoved hard against him, making him release me. *I will not give up!* I thought, determined to fight. To fight for Devon, and my friends. I took a shaky breath and thought, *No, I am fighting for everyone!*

I took a deep breath and took a step towards him, my left hand clenched around the burning cold obsidian marble, my right hand tight against the heat of my ring. I threw both hands forward and shot a stream of golden fire towards him, enveloping him in a cage of obsidian flames.

Power streaked out of me racing towards a small grove of Aspen, and I singled out one tree. That stream of golden fire fed that tree until it grew three times larger than the others, flashing through the seasons, passing decades in a matter of seconds. The spring leaves fading into summer green, then fall yellow, until the leaves dropped to the ground. Cycle after cycle, the leaves changed and the tree grew in height. The leaves gathered in a mound at the base of the tree that grew higher in seconds, with each turn of the seasons.

Avdar, in Devon's body, grew enraged behind his cage of Obsidian fire and screamed obscenities. He grabbed onto the bars of flame, yelling when his hands burned. *Devon's hands*, I thought heatedly. But he didn't have the power to break through them.

The tree stopped growing, but its leaves still waved in the wind of power I fed into it.

My mind flashed through scenes of everything I'd been through this year, my mother's death, the cross country ride alone, Brenna opening her home to me, my new friends at school, my training and friendship with Cole, my emerging feelings for Devon, all of the fights with the Daïmonids, Cole's death, and culminating with this battle against Avdar. I was furious.

A bright white light enrobed my body, my eyes rolling back in my head. I saw words scrolling through my brain and in a voice that was not my own, I began to chant:

While this battle is over
The war has just begun
The prophecy of power combined
Has been born.

He who does not belong
Has been captured
He who does not belong
Carries peace within him

Darkness and peace will reside here
Until the time has come to fight again
Good will fight against evil
And the Reign of Peace will begin.

Power shot from my body into Avdar's, capturing him in a white light. He screamed loud and long as he was carried by this white light towards the large Aspen tree where he lay spread eagle against the trunk. The power holding him pinned against it, until he slowly faded, merging with the wood, the branches of the tree wrapping around him, caging him in.

As the power subsided, my eyes opened and I looked at the tree, now petrified, its branches still wrapped around its heart. Through the branches I could see a scorch mark on the trunk in the shape of an eye.

As I stared, the blue eye blinked once, then turned orange red.

My eyes opened to the early morning sunlight glinting on the dew covered soccer field.

Acknowledgements and thanks

I have had so much help and encouragement in writing this book. First I would like to thank the *Finish the Damn Book* club mentored by Cherry Adair. It really gave me the impetus to finish this damn book!

My family have been huge supporters listening to me and reading with enthusiasm. I couldn't have done this without my husband, Derry. He gave me encouragement when I was down and helped me see my vision through. Without his IT skills I would've been lost. Love you tons!

And to you, my readers... Thank you so much for reading *Midnight Metamorphosis*! This book was several years in the making and has meant a lot to me. I would love it if you would leave a review on your favorite retailer site.

Connect with me on Twitter: *@debkehoe* or on Facebook: *DeborahEKehoe*.

www.ingramcontent.com/pod-product-compliance
Ingram Content Group UK Ltd.
Pitfield, Milton Keynes, MK11 3LW, UK
UKHW041840190726
13854UKWH00002B/640

9 781782 012146